safe
bet

safe bet

New York Times Bestselling Author
Monica Murphy

Safe Bet
Copyright © 2017 by Monica Murphy

Interior Design and formatting by

E.M.
TIPPETTS
BOOK DESIGNS

www.emtippettsbookdesigns.com

everafter ROMANCE

chapter
One

Sydney

"Okay, I feel pretentious as hell saying this, but let me explain exactly what the job description is," the pretty blonde woman says with a wince, then rolls her green eyes, a little smile teasing the corners of her mouth.

It's kind of weird, sitting across from her after I've only ever seen her on TV, the Web, or in the occasional magazine. She's much prettier in real life, and much smaller too. I just thought her husband was a total giant, but no. She's really short and thin, though kind of top heavy, if you know what I mean.

I nod but remain silent, curling my hands together in my lap. She can't see them beneath the table, and I'm glad. My fingers twist around each other, I'm so nervous. I need this job. Desperately. Trying to play it cool is becoming increasingly hard the longer I sit in front of her.

She's famous. She's beautiful. And do I really believe I have a chance to work for her and her family? Come on. I'm not that lucky.

"I've never hired a full-time live-in nanny in my life and truthfully, I don't think I need one. It goes against everything I believe in, because I actually *like* spending time with my kids. I'm trying my best to be a good mother and I don't think that involves letting other people raise my children," she explains, her gaze fixed on the piece of paper in front of her. It's a list of some sort, possibly what the job she's interviewing me for entails, yet I still say nothing. "So having you work with me is not always going to be about the children."

Um, then why are they looking for a full-time nanny?

"How old are your children?" I ask, my voice even, my expression hopefully pleasant. I have to show interest. And really, I *am* interested, even though the nanny part terrifies me. I have no experience with children. None.

Zero.

She lifts her head and smiles, her green eyes sparkling. "My daughter is four and my son is almost two. I can't lie, they're a total handful. Not that they misbehave all the time or anything, it's just that at their age, they're busy. All the time."

Nerves make my stomach clench and my mouth goes dry. Yeah, taking care of two children under the age of five is freaking scary. I can barely take care of myself, especially lately. I've cried a lot. Spent a lot of nights on friends' couches because I had nowhere to live. Didn't want to be a burden on my older brother, even though eventually I went and stayed with him and his girlfriend for a while. Gabe has done what he can, but he's busy. He has his own life to live.

I can't expect him to stop living his life just because I screwed up mine.

Everything has changed these last few months. Before I was used to doing whatever I wanted—spa treatments, going out to dinner, shopping. Paying for it all with Daddy's credit card, all without a care in the world. Then my parents found out I was lying about college. As in, I told them I was going, when I wasn't. My dad got so mad, he cut me off completely—and kicked me out of their house.

Now I'm so desperate for a job I'll try to be a freaking nanny. This is laughable. A joke. That my brother is the one who got me this interview is unbelievable. Does Gabe really think I'm capable of doing something like this? I'll probably drop the toddler on his head and his mama will fire me on the spot, then call the police and have me arrested for child abuse.

I part my lips, ready to tell her I'm totally not qualified and she should probably consider someone else for the position, when she starts speaking again.

"This is slightly embarrassing, but more than anything, I need someone to—help me." She tips her head toward me, her expression serious. "Not just with the kids, but with life. The kids keep me so busy, and so does my husband, and I can't stay focused half the time. I just need someone to help me stay organized."

"I could probably do that," I murmur, clutching my hands together. I can feel sweat start to form on the back of my neck, my entire body stiff with nerves and...anticipation? Maybe I can help her if I don't need to chase after children all the time.

"Oh, that is exactly what I needed to hear. I'm a frantic mess most of the time lately, and it stresses me out. And when I'm stressed out, my kids get stressed out, and then no one's happy." She takes a deep breath and lets it out slowly. "I'd need you to be discreet, though. Our private life is exactly that. Private. I'd need you to sign a non-disclosure agreement and everything. I hope that's okay with you."

She's talking like I already have the job. I can't be that lucky. "I don't mind. I'm here for you if you hire me. Whatever you need me to do, I'll do it. I just — I really need this job."

"Well, I really need someone to help me, so it looks like you and I could help each other." Her smile is gentle. "Trust me, most of the time I feel like I'm a total sham. So whatever you can do to make my life easier, I'm all for it."

My mouth drops open. She really believes she's a total sham? She's so poised, so calm and self-possessed. "Women all over the country admire you. You have it all. A handsome, successful husband, two beautiful children, a gorgeous house."

I look around, taking in the room we're sitting in. I assume it's her office, and it's immaculate. White and airy, it's my dream office come to life, not that I even realized I wanted a home office, considering I'm only nineteen. There are photos on every available flat surface featuring her children and husband, not that I can blame her. If I were married to that man, I wouldn't want him out of my sight. Ever. He's painfully handsome.

"Ha, you're hired." She points at me, and though she sounds like she's joking, I'm thinking she's serious. I can't help but let my hopes rise, though I tell myself to remain calm. Rational. Subdued. She doesn't want a spazzed out nanny. She needs someone she can rely on. "Seriously, sometimes I feel like my life is nothing but a dream and I'm bound to wake up one day to discover that none of this actually happened."

Should I ask? I have to ask. "Why do you say that?"

"My life wasn't always this—wonderful." Her voice turns somber, her expression sad. Her green eyes get this faraway look, like she's fallen back into the past and it's full of nothing but bad memories. "I had it hard growing up. Like, *really* hard. And I didn't always make the best choices."

"I'm thinking you made a solid choice when you met your future husband," I point out.

Her expression softens. "Oh, I didn't choose him. He chose me," she murmurs, a secretive smile curling her lips.

Lucky her. "Well, he saw something in you then. Something special." Hmm, I wonder if I said too much…

She tilts her head to the side, her long blonde hair falling over her shoulder. She looks like a fairy princess, which I guess is apt, considering her name is Fable. "I like you."

I smile, feeling all that hope rise within me once again. Maybe I do have a chance. "Thanks. I like you too."

"I think we could work well together. I have to remind you, this would be a live-in position. I'd need you here at all times because my schedule is so crazy, but you'd get time off, of course. I just—I need someone I can count on. Someone I can trust." She holds her hand out toward me, I take it, and we shake. "I'd like to offer you the job, Sydney."

Her words send shock waves coursing through my body and I try my best to contain myself. I can't believe what she just said. My entire body starts to tremble with a combination of relief and excitement. "Thank you. I'd like to accept the position."

I press my lips together, mentally warning myself not to cry. But the relief is so overwhelming, I sag the moment I let go of Fable Callahan's hand. I have a job. Somewhere I can live and eat and actually make money. I just proved my parents wrong.

I'm almost half tempted to call them and rub their faces in it.

Wade

"Your down and out attitude is bullshit." Drew claps me on the back so hard I take a stumbling step forward, thankful I don't fall flat on my face. We're in his backyard. Me pacing and grumbling, him trying to...I don't know. Talk me down off the ledge? Though right now I should feel like I'm on top of the world. I'm an ungrateful asshole and I know it.

But it's like I can't help myself. My emotions are all over the place. I even talked to my mom about it, and she told me to snap out of it.

Yeah, I lost you too, right? Whatever. Just know this:

I'm an idiot.

"You should be celebrating right now," Drew says, his expression fierce as he points a finger right at me. I'm surprised he doesn't poke me in the chest to make his point. "You made it through the initial training. The coast is pretty much clear. You'd have to royally fuck up to lose your position. I'd say there's an eighty-five percent chance you're in for the season."

It's that leftover fifteen percent that makes me nervous. Fills me with fear that I make one mistake, one wrong move, and I'm off the team.

"You've got this in the bag," Drew continues to say, all the easy confidence that makes him who he is filling his voice. I stuff the envy I'm experiencing deep down inside and try to focus on what he's telling me. "So quit whining like a pussy. You've made it."

Easy for him to say. He was a first draft pick and went on to take his team to the playoffs his rookie year. He and his team won the Super Bowl in his second season. In the eyes of the entire team—hell to practically everyone in the NFL—Drew motherfuckin' Callahan can do no wrong.

Me? I'm only just starting out. Everything can fall apart in an instant. I can't forget that.

"I haven't made it yet. There's still a chance they'll let me go." I smile but it feels bogus, so I let it fade. I know he's right. He's trying to make me feel better and I appreciate it.

I appreciate even more how easily he took me in, like I'm a member of his family. I'm not. Oh, I'm an honorary member, and Fable reminds me of that often enough that I'm forced to believe her. Her little brother Owen is my best friend. He's like a brother to me. Growing up, we were always together, and we shared a house in college.

Plus, we played football together like no other. He was always there when I needed him and vice versa. We had each other's backs, and not just on the field either. It was me and Owen Maguire against the world. Even when he met and fell in love with Chelsea, he never pushed me out of his life, while other friends had in the past. It was natural. A girl walked in, rocked their world, and friends always took a backseat.

Never with Owen and Chelsea. And while I admire — and even envy — what they have, I'm not ready to settle down. First, I'm too damn busy focusing on my career. Second, there are just too many beautiful women in this world for me to choose only one. Who needs one woman when you can have many?

Yeah. When it comes to women, sometimes I can be a... pig. But at least I'm aware of my piggish qualities, right? Chelsea says the first step is being aware of your faults, and I'm definitely aware.

I'm just not ready to correct those faults yet.

Besides, I haven't found a girl I want to be with on a steady basis, you know? I'm too young and all that shit. I like a variety of women. Thin, curvy, red hair, dark hair, blondes. Funny, serious, sexy, shy — I love them all. If I had to settle with just one woman, I know I'd go crazy.

But I consider Owen lucky, because Chelsea is amazing. She effortlessly accepted me into her life and we're close. I give Owen constant shit that she's the better part of him, and he never disagrees.

Now, though, I'm pretty certain he's pissed at me. Maybe not at me per se, but pissed at the *situation*. I have what he wants. What he wanted so damn bad for so long, but didn't get. I can't help it that he was picked higher in the draft. That the Broncos snapped him up because he's damn good and somehow, by some sort of crazy miracle, I got called up too.

"They won't let you go." Drew nods, his demeanor practically oozing confidence. "I have a feeling."

The crazy thing is, I was drafted to play for Drew's football team. I'm a part of the San Francisco 49ers. A second string wide receiver who will most likely warm a bench most of the season but hot shit, I'm a Niner. They were my favorite team growing up. Owen's too. It was his dream, to play on the same team with his brother-in-law, to keep it in the family.

Instead he's going to Denver where he gets to freeze his balls off and play *against* his brother-in-law.

Oh and possibly me. Well, if I ever get off the damn bench, that is.

"Whatever you say, bro. You said you were taking me out to celebrate tonight, right?" I ask Drew because I know he'll say yes, and then I'll most likely back out and return to my lonely apartment where I'll sulk like a baby for the rest of the night.

Which is stupid, but I can't help it. Most of the time I bluster through life without a care in the world, not paying attention to my mood and who it might affect. I just do what I want and fuck the consequences. Owen lived like that too. Every once in a while one of us grew a conscience—thanks to my mom or Fable—but otherwise, we fought against the norm.

We always believed the norm was boring, damn it. Being good, following the rules? Screw that. We wanted to have fun.

Fun can cost you, though. Our friend Des is back in our hometown selling drugs to college students and not inclined to change his career path. We couldn't save him, no matter how badly we wanted to. We had our own lives to take care of. We couldn't be Des's babysitter forever.

"Ah, that must be the girl Fable hired," Drew says, pulling me from my thoughts.

I face the same direction Drew is looking, which is toward

the large back patio. Their house is massive yet it somehow feels like how a real home should. I like hanging out here. They always make me feel welcome. "How is Fable?"

"Stressed the hell out. She has a lot on her plate. That's why she's hiring someone to help her," Drew explains, his gaze never leaving his wife.

There's another one who's madly in love with his woman. I know that they had it rough when they first got together, but their love for each other is so all-consuming, it's almost uncomfortable to witness sometimes. And I say that because I'm a dude who's definitely not in touch with my inner most feelings, if you catch my drift.

My gaze skims over the tiny but mighty Fable Maguire Callahan and lands on the girl standing next to her. She's taller than Fable, but that doesn't mean much because pretty much everyone looks tall when they're next to Fable. The girl seems young, her long, golden blonde hair pulled into a low ponytail, and she's wearing a simple black dress that skims over pretty curves. She's completely overdressed compared to Fable, who's in jeans and a pale pink T-shirt, her bright blonde hair piled on top of her head in a messy bun.

The girl glances in our direction, her gaze snagging on us, or most likely on Drew. He seems to draw that sort of attention no matter where he goes, and I'm perfectly content to remain in the background. Owen was always the bigger star in our friendship too, and I'm fine with it. Attention was never my thing.

It never has been.

"Drew!" Fable calls, waving him over. "Come meet Sydney."

He starts to head over there and when he sends me a look over his shoulder, I reluctantly follow him. I really don't need to be involved in this scenario, but I just can't tell him that, can I? It would be rude. And I'm never rude to Drew and Fable.

Ever.

"Sydney, this is my husband, Drew. Drew, this is Sydney Walker. She's going to be our new nanny," Fable says, sounding pleased. She looks over at her husband with a little wince. "I hope you don't mind that I went ahead and hired her."

"Of course I don't mind. I trust your judgment." Drew turns to greet Sydney. "Good to meet you," he says as he gives Sydney a firm handshake. She's staring up at him, her lips slightly parted, her eyes wide. Full on awestruck, which is typical. He's a superstar. That's how most people look at Drew when they first meet him.

"Hi," she squeaks, her cheeks going pink as she releases Drew's hand. Her gaze slips to mine, and then flitters away. But that one quick glance was like a sucker punch to my gut.

The nanny is beautiful.

I take a deep breath, shoving my hands in my jeans' pockets so I won't do something stupid—like try to grab her. She has pretty blue eyes and a full mouth that's made for kissing. Her curves are even lusher than I first realized. She has full hips and a tiny waist and shapely legs. But I can't worry about pretty nannies right now. I have to concentrate on work.

It still blows my mind that I might play for the NFL. That football is my job. I'm a lucky son-of-a-bitch.

"Sydney, this is Wade Knox. He's an old family friend," Fable says, knocking me from my thoughts. I blink and look down to find Sydney smiling up at me, interest clearly showing in her gaze. Hmm. "Wade, this is Sydney."

"Hey Sydney." I shake her hand, electricity pulsing between us the moment our palms touch. She jerks her hand away from mine as if I burned her. Guess she felt it too.

Interesting.

"Nice to meet you," she murmurs as she takes a step back. Like she needs the distance.

Even more interesting.

We make small talk for a few minutes before Fable takes Sydney back to the house, and the moment the door shuts behind them, Drew's talking.

"The nanny's cute," he observes, his voice way too nonchalant.

"Uh huh."

"She looked at you like she thought you were cute, too."

I roll my eyes. He never says stuff like this, so what's his deal? "Cute? What are you doing? Trying to play matchmaker?" I send him a pointed look. "Give me a break. I don't need the distraction."

He shrugs. "Nothing like the love of a good woman to keep a man on the straight and narrow especially doing what we do."

I am nowhere close to doing what he does, but I'm honored he's lumped us together. That's what I've always appreciated about Drew. He has never thought he was better than anyone else, and the guy always had reason to. He's rich, he's good looking, he's a talented quarterback, his wife is gorgeous, his kids are cute. He is living the fucking perfect life.

If I could have one-tenth of the life that he's had, I'd be happy.

And that's the truth.

chapter
TWO

Sydney

Two weeks into my job as the live-in nanny and sort of assistant to Fable and I'm freaking exhausted. Of course, I've never worked a job like this in my life ever (I've never worked a job ever, period), so that I'm still employed by the Callahans, especially after the last few days, is some sort of miracle.

Their children, while sweet and adorable and fun, are also a complete handful, just as Fable warned. Every single day, Autumn runs me ragged. She's just so fast, zipping around the house, the yard, the park, the store, wherever we're at. And she's always getting into things. Jacob is kind of needy—but he's a toddler, so I'm assuming all toddlers are needy. Plus, he really loves his mom. Like, he will full-on cry and demand to be with her the moment he spots her. When she's not around, he's content. But he catches sight of her and that's it. He forgets all about me and cries for her.

He is definitely a mama's boy.

But Fable steps in a lot and spends time with her children, just as I expected she would. She's a good mom — gentle and patient and always willing to be with them as much as she can. Nothing like I remember my mom being when I was little. She wasn't around much at all, and when she did spend time with my brother Gabe and me, it always felt like she treated us as if we were a burden, versus her actually *wanting* to be with us.

Even when I was a little kid, I could sense that.

I stopped acting star struck every time Drew came around pretty quickly. At first, I couldn't help it. I've seen him on TV countless times, on the cover *of Sports Illustrated* — heck, both of them were on the cover of *People* magazine the year the Niners won the Super Bowl. It was hard at first to wrap my head around the fact that they're real people who put their pants on one leg at a time, just like you and me. But they're very real — and so nice.

Plus, Drew is just ridiculously good looking. The two of them together are such a striking couple. All I want to do is gawk whenever I see them. Their love for each other is so obvious. They kind of remind me of my brother and his girlfriend. Gabe and Lucy are totally in love and have no problem letting the world know it either. Thankfully I adore Lucy. Otherwise, the two of them would gross me out.

You know what doesn't gross me out, though? How Drew always has his teammates over at the house when they're not at practice. Big, hulking football players are constantly coming around, seeking advice on plays, about the coaches, how to handle the constant pressure to be the best. Most of them were looking for tips or just wanted to hang out. And Drew was always gracious. He never seemed to mind his teammates coming by.

Neither did I.

I had no idea I was drawn to big, beefy football players before. Those types of guys were never my thing. In high school, I didn't pay attention to the jocks. I thought they were obnoxious jerks most of the time. But these guys who play on Drew's team, they're gorgeous. And they seem nice too, especially one in particular.

Wade Knox.

He's at the house right now, sitting outside by the pool and chatting with Drew, their expressions deadly serious. I'm standing in front of the sink in the kitchen, rinsing out sippy cups before I set them in the dishwasher and staring out the window over the sink that faces the backyard.

Spying on them, I guess. I can't help it. Wade is always around, yet I never really get a chance to talk to him. I only know a few facts, and these I've gleaned from Fable without being too obvious I'm digging for information. But I do know this:

He's Fable's brother's best friend.

He's twenty-two years old.

He's a newly chosen wide receiver for the 49ers.

He's single.

Fable thinks the world of him.

I let the warm water run over my hands as I stare out the window, my gaze locked on Wade. He's tall and broad and muscular. His dark brown hair is overgrown, like he needs a haircut but doesn't care enough to get one. But the look works for him, because his hair curls around his gorgeous face and the back of his neck, and it looks soft. Makes me want to touch it.

His eyes are brown and warm, and he has this intense way when he looks at me. Like he sees right through me, which is sort of intimidating and exhilarating, all at once. He's big and broad, with shoulders as wide as a mountain and arms that look like they could crush me if he squeezed just a little too hard. His mouth is full but he doesn't smile often enough, and he has a jawline that looks like it could cut glass, it's so sharp.

"Hey, isn't California currently in major drought conditions?"

Fable's teasing voice breaks through my thoughts, and I hurriedly shut off the water, embarrassed that I got caught watching the guys outside. "Sorry. Got distracted," I mumble as I open the dishwasher and set all of the sippy cups and their lids in the top rack.

"Understandable." Fable leans against the kitchen counter, smiling at me. "Please tell me you were checking out Wade."

"I wasn't," I automatically say. I don't want her to think I'm only here to ogle all the guys that are constantly hanging around. It's definitely an unexpected benefit, but I don't want her to think poorly of me. "I was just…staring off into space. And thinking." I shut the dishwasher door and grab a towel, quickly wiping down the sink before I throw the towel in the dish drain.

"Uh huh." The knowing smirk on her face makes me feel guilty. "Wade is single, you know."

"No, I didn't know." I'm sure girls throw themselves at Wade on a constant basis. He's a newly minted professional football player. The world is his oyster or however that dumb saying goes. He could have anyone he wants—he's that good looking. I'm a nobody. A dumb girl who's made a lot of mistakes and is now paying for them by having to get a job and take care of herself rather than rely on her parents' money.

Though supposedly that's going to make me stronger— at least, according to my parents. But right now, I don't feel stronger. I feel weak and useless and I worry most of the time I got this job only out of pity. The Callahans only interviewed me as a favor for a friend of a friend of my brother's.

Sad but true.

"He's such a good guy, though he's never really had someone steady in his life—a girlfriend," Fable continues. Both of her children are napping and that's when we usually talk. Or we go to her office and try to organize her schedule, which is a big job considering she practically lives and dies by her schedule. She's a planner, and I get it. With everything on her plate, she needs to be. But we're easily distracted. Sometimes we get right down to business, and other times we gossip a little bit, though right now she seems to want to talk about...

Wade.

And I'm not going to protest, though I probably should. I need to keep this business only. I don't want to cause any problems by possibly flirting with Wade. Not like he's shown any interest. He wouldn't bother with someone like me.

Honestly, I'm totally reaching.

"I'm sure doing what he does, he probably doesn't want

one," I tell her, and when she sends me a blank look, I add, "A girlfriend."

"Oh. Yes. Well, I'm sure you're right. He's just starting on his career and that's usually when they have to fight off the women, especially a guy as good looking as Wade. Or maybe he's just been waiting to find the right one, you know?" The smile she sends my way almost implies I could be the right one for Wade, which is impossible.

I'm not. I'm a complete mess. Plus, I'm too young and I don't know what I want or need and oh my God, I sound like my parents right now. Like the lecture they've been giving me over the last few years has totally sunk in and my thoughts are filled with their disapproval.

Ugh. Maybe I am young, but I'm also an adult. I need to start acting like one and not letting what my parents think of me shape who I'm becoming.

"I'm guessing he has no desire to find a steady girlfriend right now. And I'm not looking for a steady boyfriend either," I tell Fable, my voice firm. I don't want her getting any ideas that I'm interested in Wade. I'm really not. I don't even know him. Besides, I want her to take me seriously. This is my job. I don't want to flirt with a hot guy while I'm working. Yes, it's a perk to have football players around all the time, but that's all it is. A perk. I can look, but I can't touch.

Now Fable's frowning, and I feel like I've said the wrong thing. "Yes, fine. You're probably right. I always want to put people together, I swear. Drew says I need to stop my matchmaking ways, but I can't help it. I want people to be as happy as we are."

Aw, that's sweet. I soften a little bit at her words because I can see she genuinely means it. But we all can't have the perfect life that Drew and Fable Callahan have. What they share is rare and beautiful and we could all be so lucky to have a love like theirs.

"I just worry. Wade is having a rough time. Practice has been tough and his confidence seems low. He's afraid he's going to get cut from the team, and Drew has been giving him a lot of pep talks lately to keep him encouraged," Fable explains.

"Is he a good player?"

"He's a great player, but his confidence is shaky." Fable's smile is gentle. "It's normal for players to go through tumultuous emotions when they first start. Everything's on the line and they're so close to making their dreams come true. Sometimes they fail, though. And that's hard for them to process. They want to believe in the fairytale."

"What fairytale?"

"That they'll all go on to win Super Bowl rings and championships and be the greatest player that ever lived. That's not always guaranteed. You have to put in hard work first and make it happen, you know? You have to want it bad enough." Fable's gaze drifts to the window and locks on the two men still sitting outside. "Wade doesn't just want it for himself, though. He wants it for his mom too. He wants to make sure she's taken care of for the rest of her life, though I know he's secretly afraid he won't make it and he'll disappoint her."

How sweet. He wants to take care of his mom. Most guys are selfish and only care about themselves.

"Sometimes he acts like making it on the team isn't that

important to him, but deep down inside, he wants it. I know he does. He's working hard toward it too. He'll cement his spot on the team, but he just needs to build up more of his confidence first."

I glance out the window once again, letting my gaze wander to the two men sitting by the pool outside. The day is clear and bright, the temperature unusually warm for San Francisco. They're both wearing black shorts and red 49ers T-shirts, the cotton stretching taut across their broad shoulders, the sunlight gleaming off their dark heads. Their expressions are serious, Wade's more earnest than anything else as he hunches forward, as if in rapt attention over whatever Drew is telling him.

Taking a deep breath, I return my attention to Fable, smiling at her. "Is there anything you want me to help you with today while the kids are sleeping?"

"I'm so glad you asked, or I probably would've forgot. There's too much going on and not enough hours in the day to get it all done." Fable's expression brightens. "Let's go to my office. We can go through that fat stack of mail sitting on my desk."

We both groan, then she starts to laugh. I definitely need to focus on something else, and sorting through her mail is better than daydreaming about Wade Knox.

Wade

"Fable's probably sick of seeing me hanging around here all the time, huh?" I mutter as I follow Drew back inside the house.

"Nah. She loves having you around. You're the closest

thing to Owen and she misses him so damn bad. If she can't have him nearby, at least she has you," Drew tells me as he shuts the French door that leads into the kitchen. He glances at the giant clock that hangs on the nearby wall. "I'm freaking starving. Want to go grab some dinner?"

"Uh..." My voice drifts. I don't want to take up all of Drew's time. But I also don't want to go back to my boring, empty apartment in San Jose. I live close to the stadium because it's easier to get to practice every day. Drew bought a badass house in San Francisco a couple of years ago because he's a multimillionaire and can afford it. So what if his commute to work is longer than mine? His house makes it worth the drive every day.

"We'll go grab some pizza or something. Make it easy," Drew says.

"Did someone say pizza?" Fable walks into the kitchen, Jacob propped on her right hip. He has a fistful of Fable's hair and he's staring at it in fascination. "I'm hungry. Let's go somewhere."

"Yeah, but where?" Drew drops a kiss on Fable's upturned lips when she stops to stand beside him. He then takes Jacob from her arms and cuddles him close. "You really want pizza?"

"I adore pizza. You know this. You fed it to me constantly during your college days." The knowing look she sends Drew has him kissing her again. I feel like I'm intruding during a private moment, so I look away. "You're going with us too, right Wade?"

"If you don't mind." I don't want to be a third wheel.

Fable beams. "Perfect. I'll ask if Sydney wants to go with us too."

Wait a minute. I won't be a third wheel. It'll be more like we're on a—double date? I don't know how I feel about that. I don't know how Sydney's going to feel about it either.

I mean, the girl is hot, but she works for Drew and Fable. She's the freaking nanny. Which means I shouldn't have dirty thoughts about her, though I do. I wonder if her skin is as soft as it looks, and her hair. What her lips might taste like....

Yeah, the nanny is gorgeous. Quiet and pretty, with a soft yet sexy laugh and those beautiful blue eyes. I've been checking her out. And I swear she's been checking me out too. So going to pizza together tonight could be potentially awkward.

I'm willing to give it a shot, though.

"Fable." Drew's voice is low, carrying a warning with it.

"What? It's no big deal. We'll be four—*friends* going out for a meal." Fable's expression is full on innocent and also full on bullshit.

I love Fable, but I've known her too long. I can see right through her. I think she's trying to set me up with the nanny.

Interesting.

"Sydney's not your friend. She's your employee." Drew steps closer to his wife, reaching out so he can skim his fingers up and down her bare arm. "Maybe you should be careful about crossing lines and all that."

"But I really like her. So do the kids. A nanny is supposed to be a part of our family, right? So we're going out to dinner as a family, along with our family friend Wade, and Sydney is going to accompany us. She'll be a huge help with the kids. So what's the big deal?"

Drew sighs. "Fine. No big deal. Let's go eat pizza then. Need help rounding up everything?"

Fable looks like she wants to hop up and down like a little kid, she's so happy. "No, I've got this. Sydney will help me." She turns her gaze on me, grinning from ear to ear. "You *are* coming with us, right Wade?"

"Oh, yeah," I drawl, flashing Fable a smile.

I wouldn't miss this pizza date for the world.

The pizza place is called Fire, and it's one of those trendy, out of the way restaurants that's full of people decked out in their best designer clothes, where I probably look like a slob in my athletic shorts and T-shirt, though I really don't give a shit. Drew's wearing the same damn thing, but the employees are practically bowing at his feet like he's a king and they're all his measly servants.

Not that he acts like that, but it's kind of wild, how he commands everyone's attention no matter where he goes.

The owner comes right out to greet us when he discovers the Callahans are dining at his restaurant tonight, and they find us a table in a discreet corner immediately. Both Autumn and Jacob are in good spirits since they just woke up from a long nap, and Sydney is tending to them, sending a shy smile my way every once in a while. Otherwise, she's not really saying a word to any of us beyond the kids. Drew finally takes Autumn from her since she keeps trying to make her escape and run through the restaurant.

"This place is packed," I mention to Fable as we both check out our menus. Drew is holding Autumn, who won't stop squirming. That she can almost sneak out of her dad's strong arms is saying something.

"Lots of local celebrities come to this place," Fable says, her gaze never leaving the menu in front of her. "It's usually quiet and you can eat here without worrying about the paparazzi."

I scan the room. It's wall to wall with people, every table and chair filled, along with the bar. There's outdoor dining as well, and it looks packed too. There was a line out the door when we arrived, so I'm guessing the word is out. "I think your quiet restaurant where you can eat privately is no more."

A worried expression appears immediately on Fable's face. "That's too bad. I love this place. I love their salads."

"So there are local celebrities here?" Sydney looks around the restaurant with wide eyes, hoping she can spot one, I assume. She's holding a fussy Jacob in her arms and he's clutching a handful of her hair in his fist.

"Mostly athletes. Sometimes local news personalities show up. People like that." Fable leans in close, her gaze never leaving Sydney's. "I saw Joe Montana with his family the last time we were here."

Sydney frowns. "Who's that?"

"Oh God." I rest my hand on my chest, shocked at her sacrilegious question. "Please tell me you're joking."

"Um…I can tell you that, but I'm really not." She winces.

Drew starts to laugh, shaking his head. "You're serious?" he asks her.

"Who is he?" Sydney turns to Fable for help.

"Only the greatest quarterback to ever play for the Niners—and maybe the entire NFL," I answer for Fable.

Sydney turns her pretty blue gaze on me. "When did he play?"

"Throughout the '80s. He won four Super Bowls."

She smiles. "Well, there you go. I wasn't even born in the '80s, so how I would I know who he is?"

"I wasn't born in the '80s either," I answer. I notice Fable and Drew are talking menu choices, so I decide to ask Sydney a personal question. "How old are you?"

"Nineteen." Her cheeks turn the faintest pink, as if she's embarrassed to admit her age.

Because damn, the girl is young. Well, only three years younger than me, but still. It feels like a huge difference considering where I'm at in my life and where she's at in hers.

She can't even walk into a bar legally. Not that I've gone out much since I've come here. I'm trying to leave all that behind. In college, we partied all the time. Me, Owen and Des. Until we got out of control and Owen nearly ruined his relationship with Chelsea—hell, at one point, he almost got kicked off the football team. Getting high all the time wasn't doing any of us any favors. So I quit, and so did Owen. Considering I'm in training right now, I won't even touch a beer.

"Have you been a nanny before?" I ask her.

Sydney shakes her head. "This is my first job ever."

I raise my brows. "Seriously?" She nods, doesn't say a word. "How did you meet Fable?"

"Mutual friend. My brother knows her brother."

That was a vague answer.

"Your brother knows Owen?" When she nods, I continue. "How exactly? Maybe I know your brother too."

"I doubt it." She smiles. "They met through Owen's girlfriend, I think? She was participating in a summer program at the same college my brother goes to and they somehow crossed paths. I think at a party."

"Wild." I shake my head. "It can be a pretty freaking small world sometimes, I swear."

"I know, right? I've never met Owen though, or his girlfriend."

"They're cool." I pause. "You'd like them."

There's that shy smile again. "I'm sure." She looks away, like she's a little embarrassed and I smile to myself.

Only for the smile to quickly fade.

She's hella cute, but completely off limits. I can't go thinking I can mess around with the sexy nanny—Drew and Fable's employee, when I should be focused on football and training and hoping like hell the coaches won't cut me loose. I don't want to go home a loser. I promised my mom I'd do this. I promised her I'd take care of her for the rest of her life. I want to live up to that promise too. Whatever it takes.

I can't screw up.

chapter Three

Wade

"I don't feel so good."

I glance up to see Fable watching me, her gaze vacant, her face pale. She blinks at me, like she's trying to bring me into focus but can't quite do so. My heart immediately starts to race. "You don't look so good either," I tell her.

She gives me a wan smile just before she grimaces, touching her forehead with splayed fingers. "My head is spinning."

We'd pretty much finished eating about fifteen minutes ago, but we're lingering because the kids were having fun in the retro video game room with Drew, though usually that's where the hipsters hang out. He was sitting at one of those racecar games with Jacob on his lap and Autumn running circles around him, screaming for him to go faster. Sydney had made her quick escape to the bathroom, leaving me alone with Fable.

Who's suddenly not feeling well.

Don't panic, dude.

"Are you all right?" I ask.

Fable shakes her head, then winces. "I don't know. I feel really lightheaded. Maybe I should go to the bathroom and splash some water on my face."

"Should I go get Drew?"

"No, I can walk to the bathroom like a big girl. I'll be all right." She mutters it again under her breath. "I'll be all right," but she doesn't sound like herself. Her attempt at humor falls flat. She's acting strange.

"Come on, Fable. Are you sure you don't want me to help you?" I study her face. Man, she's pale. Even her lips are white. It's like all the color has been leeched from her face, and along with her pale blonde hair, she reminds me of a ghost.

"Yeah. No. I'll be fine." She tries to stand but practically falls back into her chair. I leap from mine and go around to stand behind her, resting my hands lightly on her shoulders. I don't want her to get up again on her own. What if she falls? She could hurt herself. "I'm going to go get Drew."

"No." She glances at me from over her shoulder, resting her cold hand on top of mine. "He'll just freak out and maybe scare the kids. Please, Wade, just—help me to the bathroom." She tries to smile reassuringly, but it doesn't work.

The scared expression on her face just freaks me out even more.

I help her get up from her chair, shocked when she stumbles a little and falls into me. She rights herself, shooting me a weak smile, and I clutch her arm as we weave through the crowded tables toward the bathroom, which is on the other side of the building.

Of course.

"It's so warm in here," she murmurs as she presses against my side. "I don't know why my head is spinning."

I wrap my arm lightly around her waist, hoping no one notices. I don't want people to think I'm trying to make a play on Drew's wife. Talk about a scandal. "You're going to be fine." My voice is firm, though deep inside, I'm panicking. I forgot my freaking phone in Drew's car and was too lazy to go out and grab it earlier. Otherwise I'd be dialing 9-1-1 right about now. Something's not right with Fable. She's acting weird and she looks terrible. "Have you ever felt like this before?"

"Um…" Her voice drifts and she makes a face, her brows lowered. "I don't remember."

Great. I wish I could find Drew. The game room is on the other side of the restaurant, near the front, and I can't abandon Fable now. I need to get her to the bathroom. Maybe we'll run into Sydney and she can help us out.

We make it back to the tiny hallway that leads to the bathrooms when I feel her lean too heavily into my side. All of her weight sags against me and I grab hold of her tightly but she slips out of my arms and onto the floor in a boneless heap.

"Fable!" I yell sharply but she doesn't respond.

She's sprawled on the floor, completely unconscious.

A door swings open and Sydney's magically there, standing right at Fable's feet. "Oh my God! Is she okay?" she asks, her voice filled with panic.

I fall to my knees and cradle Fable's head in my lap, barely looking at Sydney. "Go get Drew. Now," I snap as I touch

Fable's face, pressing firmly against her cheek. "Fable, wake up. *Fable*." I keep repeating her name, but she doesn't respond. I can tell she's breathing, but I don't know why she fainted like that. And it's freaking me the hell out.

"O-okay." Sydney takes off out of the hallway and I stare down at Fable's face. She looks like she's sleeping. Her eyes are shut, her lips parted, her face still eerily pale. I smack her cheek lightly, not wanting to hurt her, but desperate to get her to wake up.

Hell. This isn't good. What if something's wrong with her? What if she's having some sort of medical emergency? I should've had Sydney call 9-1-1 first. What the hell was I thinking? Now I'm alone in this hall in a crowded restaurant with no goddamn phone and an unconscious woman lying in my lap. The same woman who watched out for me when we were kids and I was always up to no good. Yet she never held that against me. Ever.

I owe Fable everything. I owe Drew everything too.

Icy cold fear races through me and I glance around, looking for someone. Anyone. But I don't want to cause a scene either. Drew and Fable are private people. They'll do the occasional media spread to please the press, but otherwise, they try their best to remain out of the limelight. The last thing I want to do is call attention to a potential health problem.

Fuck, I don't know what to do.

Sydney

I find Drew in the video game room, smiling and laughing

at something his daughter said. He's hauling his tall body out of the racecar game seat, clutching Jacob to him as Autumn bounces up and down near his feet, shouting "Daddy!" over and over again. He spots the panicked expression on my face and immediately rushes toward me.

"What's wrong?" he asks, his voice low.

"It's Fable," I whisper. "She fainted over by the bathrooms. Wade is with her, though."

He shoves Jacob in my arms and takes off, calling over his shoulder, "Stay with Sydney, Autumn. Daddy will be right back."

I turn to look at Autumn, who's watching me with big green eyes that match her mother's. I didn't even notice the purple lollipop she's sucking on. She's clutching the tiny stick tightly, her lips wrapped around the purple candy, her face smeared with it. I bet she's a sticky mess. "Where'd Daddy go?" she asks once she pulls the sucker out of her mouth.

"Um, he had to use the potty," I tell her. So lame, but what else could I tell her? That her mommy fainted?

I don't think so.

She starts to bounce up and down again and sings a song. "Potty time, potty time, everybody go potty time. I need to go too, Sydney. Can you take me?"

Oh. Crap. Fable fainted right in front of the bathrooms. I can't take Autumn back there. No way can she see her mom like that, passed out on the floor. I'm doing my best not to freak out, and I know Autumn will lose it if she spots her mom unconscious.

"Give me a minute." I jiggle Jacob in my arms, who's starting to fuss. "Let's see when Daddy comes back."

"But I really have to goooooo." She's still hopping, the sucker in her mouth, her hand covering her crotch, like if she lets go she'll pee everywhere. And who knows? She just might. "Right now. Right *now*."

I'm in full-blown panic mode now. I glance over my shoulder to see if anyone's emerging from the dark hall that leads to the bathrooms, but I see no one. What if something's seriously wrong with Fable? I should call 9-1-1. I should tell someone else to call 9-1-1 for me. I can't just stand here and try to manage their children. This is freaking *serious*.

God, I feel so helpless, and I think of my parents. How they never taught me to take care of myself. How they always had someone taking care of me, though it usually wasn't them. It was a nanny or a servant. The housekeeper or the driver they hired when we were younger. That guy drove us to school every day, and he watched over us too. It wasn't until I was thirteen did my brother Gabe finally tell me he was a bodyguard.

I don't know what it's like to take care of myself. But I do know this: the world is pretty freaking scary when you're on your own.

"Hey." I turn to find Drew standing in front of me and I sag in relief. I've never been so glad to see someone in my entire life. "We need to go outside and get the car."

"We do?" I frown.

"Yeah." Drew steps closer, his voice low as he says, "Fable's fine. She just woke up, was a little disoriented, but otherwise she seems fine. But I don't want to make a big scene, and neither does she. So bring the kids with you and let's go out to the car.

We'll load them up, drive around to the back of the restaurant and pick up Fable and Wade. Then we'll get out of here."

I nod, not bothering to say anything else as I grab hold of Autumn's sticky hand. "Let's go, sweetie."

"But I gotta go potty," she starts to protest as I lead her out of the game room, following after her father.

"I'll let you have another sucker if you wait a little bit." Drew kneels down to look her in the eye, his big hands engulfing her shoulders.

"You will?" Autumn breathes, those green eyes wide with wonder.

"I will. I know how much you love those things, but Daddy needs you to wait a few minutes before you can go potty. Okay? Can you do that for Daddy?"

"I can, Daddy! I can! I'm a big girl," Autumn says excitedly.

We go to our table and I grab the diaper bag, slinging it over my free shoulder. Jacob protests as I jostle him in my arms, but otherwise he's fine. I grab Autumn's hand once again and follow after Drew as we make our escape out of the restaurant.

The moment we're outside, a barrage of flashing lights hits us, one after the other. I try to dash behind Drew, but he slips his arm around my shoulders, guiding me around the side of the building toward the parking lot.

The photographers won't stop screaming at him, and they have a lot of probing questions.

"Who's the girl, Drew?"

"Does your wife know about this little date?"

"You brought your *kids*?"

"Is this the new nanny, Callahan?"

"Where's Fable?"

"Where's your wife?"

"Drew! Is it true that you and Fable are separating?"

"Is that your new girlfriend?"

Oh God. I can't turn back. I don't look at anyone. Drew removes his arm from around my shoulder and takes my hand, leading me to the car. I keep my gaze focused on his broad back, ignoring the reporters' voices, the flash of their cameras.

How do celebrities cope with this sort of thing day after day? It's awful.

As soon as the vehicle comes into view, Drew hits the keyless remote. I hurry over and put the children into their car seats, buckling them in, relieved when they're secure so I can hurriedly close the door.

"Get in the car," Drew demands and I run around the back of the car. But my foot gets caught on something and I trip, squealing as I fall onto the ground, landing heavily on my knees.

Drew appears in an instant, and I lift my head, tears threatening to fall from my eyes. Before I can say anything, he grabs hold of my arms and hauls me onto my feet. "You all right?" His gaze bores into mine, his dark brows furrowed and I nod, unable to find words.

Afraid if I try to talk, I'll end up crying instead.

He lets go of me just as the paparazzi reappears, their flashbulbs blinding as they go off again and again. I stumble once more, my back hitting the SUV and Drew grabs hold of me, scooping me up into his arms and clutching me close to his chest. The reporters become extremely loud and I know it's because of the way Drew's holding me.

In his arms. Like I'm the one who just fainted, not his wife. Which of course, the reporters don't know about any of that. They can't.

This isn't going the way we planned.

Drew throws open the door and practically shoves me into the SUV, slamming the door extra hard. He doesn't say a word as he climbs into the driver's seat and heads for the back of the restaurant. He throws the car in park and gets out, disappearing through a door that I assume leads into the restaurant. Within minutes he's back outside, Fable in his arms and looking pale, but otherwise all right.

The photographers are — of course — nowhere to be found.

"Are you okay?" I ask her once she's settled in the passenger side seat.

Fable nods, her expression still dazed. "I fainted."

"We're going to the hospital," Drew says firmly as he slides behind the steering wheel and throws the car into drive.

"Where's Wade?" I ask just as the door is thrown open and he climbs inside, sitting next to me.

"I'm right here," he says with a charming smile, one I can't help but return.

"Yay, Wade, you made it! If I can hold my pee pee for a few minutes, Daddy is going to give me another lollipop!" Autumn yells, her voice scratchy.

Drew laughs. So does Fable. Wade chuckles too.

But I don't laugh. Nope. Instead, I burst into tears.

Wade

Ah man, she's crying. I don't do well with women and tears. My mom wasn't much of a crier, she was too tough for that most of the time. But when she did actually cry? I always ended up terrified, unsure of how to comfort her. Tears make me uncomfortable.

Sydney's quiet tears are shredding me.

"Hey. Don't cry," I say quietly as I scoot closer to her and slip my arm around her shoulders, trying to offer comfort. Her entire body is stiff and she quickly wipes at her cheeks, then brushes her hair away from her face before she turns those big blue eyes on me. They're shining with unshed tears and her cheeks are splotchy, but otherwise, she looks fine.

"I'm okay," she murmurs. "I don't want to scare the kids. And they have enough to deal with." She waves a hand toward the front of the car.

I tilt my head to the right, studying Drew's profile. His jaw is tight and his mouth is grim but otherwise, he appears to have everything under control. He's not driving like a maniac, but he is going fast, which I can't blame him for that. I'd want to get to the hospital ASAP too. He says something to his wife and I tune them out, not wanting to invade their privacy.

Instead, I focus my attention on Sydney, who's got her arms wrapped around her middle and is staring out the window. "Are you sure you're really all right?" I ask, careful to keep my voice low. I don't want anyone else to hear me, just her.

She nods and turns to face me, nibbling on her lower lip.

It's a sexy look, her teeth digging into that plump bottom lip, though I know that's not what she's going for. She dashes her fingers under her eyes again, catching the last of the tears before she offers me a reassuring smile. "I'm fine. Thank you for asking."

"That was scary as hell."

"Yeah, it was." Amusement laces her tone, which I take as a good sign.

"You handled yourself pretty well."

"I'm glad you think so." She rolls her eyes. "Trust me, I was barely keeping it together."

"Same." I smile, like we share a secret. "Deep down inside I was in full on panic mode."

"Me too." Her smile softens, then completely disappears. "You'll never believe what happened when Drew and I and the kids left the restaurant earlier."

"What?"

"There were photographers out front, asking all sorts of questions. Like where was Fable, and who was I. They even mentioned me being the nanny, like they already knew. It was weird."

"Paparazzi, I guess." I don't know what that's like. No one knows me, no one cares enough about me to chase my ass out of a restaurant and flash their cameras in my face. That happens to Drew and Fable on occasion, though—tonight wasn't a good night for it, that's for sure.

Turns out that'll be the understatement of the century.

chapter
Four

Sydney

"Thank you for taking us home," I say quietly as Wade puts the SUV in park and shuts off the engine. We just arrived at the Callahan house and I'm so tired, I can barely keep my eyes open. But I can feel his gaze on me, studying me, probably ready to ask some question I can't or don't want to answer just yet, so I keep my head averted. Too afraid of what I might see if I did happen to meet his gaze.

Disappointment maybe? I know I'm definitely disappointed over how I acted. I truly believed I wouldn't crack under pressure, but seeing Fable unconscious on the floor at the restaurant just about did me in. I tried my best to keep it together and I held up for the most part. Thanks to Wade, if I'm being honest with myself. He offered comfort, and then he distracted me, which was a good thing.

A really good thing.

Though in the back of my mind, I worried constantly that entire ride to the hospital. About Fable, most definitely. I just hoped that she was okay. But I also worried about myself. About my capabilities when it came to my job. Clearly, I was unable to handle major stress. What if Drew and Fable realize that and fire me? Where would I go? What would I do?

I told myself to quit worrying about losing my job and focused on actually *doing* my job. Luckily enough, Jacob fell asleep fast. Someone dug up a lollipop for Autumn and she sucked on that thing all the way home, until she finally crashed out about ten minutes ago.

So now it's just Wade and I, and the two sleeping Callahan children. Jacob is softly snoring and he sounds adorable, but I can't truly focus on the adorableness. I'm still too caught up in my chaotic emotions.

"You're welcome," he finally says, his deep, slightly rough voice sending a ripple of awareness down my spine. "Are you all right? After everything that happened?"

"I'm fine," I say with false brightness and a careless shrug.

When he remains quiet, I can tell he's not falling for my bullshit.

"I'm okay," I say, turning to look at him. He's watching me, his gaze meeting mine, and I try to offer a reassuring smile. "Really."

"I was sort of mean to you earlier. At the restaurant." He hesitates. "And I'm sorry."

"Oh, you were fine. I totally understand. It all happened so fast." I wave a hand, brushing off his apology, his supposed rudeness. I don't remember him being mean, but maybe he was? I'm not sure. Everything is still sort of a blur.

The doubtful expression on his face tells me he still doesn't believe me, but I can't worry about this right now. I need to get Jacob and Autumn inside and into their beds. And I'm not looking forward to dealing with two cranky kids who will most likely want their mama once they realize she's not around.

Ugh.

"You need help with Autumn and Jacob? Getting them to bed?" he asks, like he can read my mind.

I nod, nibbling on my lower lip. This means I will be alone with him in the house for hours—possibly the entire night. What if the hospital doesn't release Fable right away? I'd fully expect Drew to stay by his wife's side…

You can handle this, Syd. This is your job now. You're a big girl, so act like one, damn it.

"That would be great, thanks," I murmur, glancing over my shoulder to check on the children. They both look so content, like little angels. Soon-to-be little angry angels who won't like being awoken out of a deep sleep, I bet.

Wade reaches up to push the controller to open the garage door. My gaze snags on his muscular arm, the bulging curve of his biceps. Those broad shoulders and his wide chest…the man is built. Thick and strong and I can only imagine what he must look like with his shirt off. How it would feel, to have him hold me close. Touch me. Pick me up and carry me to his…

Yeah. Scratch that. My wicked fantasies need to take a break. I have too much work to do.

Without a word we climb out of the SUV and he grabs

Autumn out of her car seat while I unbuckle Jacob. I grab the diaper bag and Wade follows me into the house, a drowsy Autumn in his arms while I hold a still sleeping Jacob.

"Where's my lollipop?" Autumn asks sleepily.

"You already ate it," Wade reminds her.

"No I didn't," she protests just as I flick on the kitchen light and turn to look at the two of them.

The lollipop stick is stuck in Autumn's fine dark brown hair, right by her ear. Her cheeks are shiny — most likely with lollipop-flavored slobber — and there are bits of red candy lingering in the corners of her mouth. "Um, I'm pretty sure you did finish the lollipop, though some of it is stuck on your face," I say.

Autumn smacks her fingers against her sticky cheeks, then glances up at Wade. "Will you give me a bath, Uncle Wade?" She blinks up at him with extra wide eyes, her lower lip trembling, like she's about to cry.

"I'm guessing Sydney will want to do that," Wade says, sounding nervous.

"No, no, no. I want you Wade. Please, please, please?" Autumn literally bats her eyelashes at him.

She's good. And she's only four.

"Let's make a deal," I say to Autumn after Wade shoots me a terrified look. "I'll put Jacob to bed while you pick out a nightgown. Then I'll start your bath and Wade can help us. Sounds good?"

Autumn nods, her smile big. She appears awfully pleased with herself. "Sounds *great*." She glances up at Wade once more. "Will you help me pick out my nightgown?"

"Sure," he says easily, though I get the distinct feeling he's uncomfortable with the entire situation. I'd bet money he doesn't interact with small children very often.

Autumn squirms in his arms and he sets her on his feet. She shoots off, giggling as she calls over her shoulder, "Come on, Uncle Wade, come on!"

His freaked out gaze meets mine and I shrug, unable to contain my amusement. "You heard her. Go on, *Uncle* Wade."

He offers me a sheepish smile and then follows Autumn. I fall into step after them, my gaze snagging on Wade's perfect butt. I mean seriously, the man has such a perfect body he probably makes angels weep with joy. My fingers literally itch to reach out and touch him.

But I don't. Instead, I take a still-sleeping Jacob to his room, where I quickly change him and tuck him into bed. He never really wakes up and I'm thankful. He may get fussy when his mom isn't around, but once he falls asleep, he's usually out for the night.

Thank goodness.

Once I finish with Jacob, I go to the kids' bathroom and start up the water in the tub, adding some bubble bath liquid. Autumn drags Wade into the room within minutes of my arrival, a pleased expression on her face. "I picked my Cinderella nightgown," she says, waving it at me.

"Good choice." I nod my approval and take the thin gown from her, placing it on the counter. "We should brush your hair first before you get into the bath, don't you think?"

She frowns and props her elbows on the marble counter. Our gazes meet in the mirror's reflection and she pouts. "Do I have to?"

"We need to get the stick out of your hair," I remind her.

Autumn tugs it out of her baby fine hair with a grimace and then hands it up to me. "Ta da! I did it, Sydney! All by myself!"

The stick has strands of wispy brown hair stuck to it. I take it from her and deposit it in the tiny trashcan. "Good job." I'm really glad she didn't pull more hair out of her head.

She giggles. "It wasn't hard. I just wanted to help."

"And you're a great helper, so thank you." I smile at her, then offer one to Wade. He crosses his arms in front of his wide chest, his eyes sparkling with amusement as he studies me.

I wonder if he likes what he sees.

Wade continues watching us as he leans against the doorjamb while Autumn and I talk. She's a decent conversationalist, with always something to say and I listen to her as I finish brushing her hair. She sheds her clothes and hops into the bathtub, giggling when the bubbles I poured in earlier puff up around her.

I just finish washing her hair when my phone rings. My hands are completely submersed in the water and my phone is in the back pocket of my jeans, so I can't really answer it. I look over my shoulder, my gaze meeting Wade's.

"Want me to get that?" he asks, his eyebrows rising.

"Um, my phone is in my back pocket." My cheeks go hot just saying it, which is so stupid. But he flusters me. His nearness, the way he's quietly observing us, I can't help but wonder what he's thinking.

"I'll grab it for you." He comes toward the tub, kneels down behind me and slowly slips my phone out of my jeans' pocket, his fingers brushing against my backside, his fingers seeming to trail across my jeans.

Did he touch me extra slow on purpose? Am I imagining things, or did his fingers seem to linger? I'm suddenly hyper aware of his close proximity, how he just touched me so intimately…

Okay, I need to get over myself. He grabbed my phone for me, for the love of God. He's trying to help me out. That's it. I'm totally overreacting.

Totally.

I turn away from him, focusing on Autumn as she wiggles her fingers in the water, making it ripple. I hear Wade as he rises to his feet, shifting so he's standing right next to me and I glance over at him.

"It's Drew," Wade says when he spots the name flashing across the screen. "Want me to answer it?"

"Please," I say just as Autumn screams, "Daddy!" and smacks the water with the palms of her hands, splashing it onto my chest. My T-shirt immediately clings to my breasts, making me look like a lame wet T-shirt contest entrant.

Great.

Wade answers my phone, quiet as he listens to whatever Drew's telling him. He then pulls the phone away from his ear and points it toward me. "He wants to talk to you."

I dry my hands on a towel and go to Wade. He hands me the phone, our fingers brushing, his gaze dropping to my wet chest for the briefest moment. I know he just checked out my chest. What did he think?

Ugh, I shouldn't care what he thinks. Nothing is going to

happen between us, right? I need to focus on my job and not the muscular, sexy football player who's eating up all the space of this decent sized bathroom just with his mere presence.

Pushing all thoughts of Wade's eyes on my boobs and his hands on my butt aside, I bring the phone to my ear and listen to Drew.

"She's fine. They're running a few tests, making sure she's all right, and then they'll most likely release her. Hopefully we won't be here for too much longer," he explains.

"Hold on." I look at Wade. "Keep an eye on Autumn, will you?" I say before I resume my conversation with Drew. "Do they know what's wrong?" I head for the bathroom doorway, needing the distance. I don't want Autumn to overhear my conversation and get worried about her mom.

"They have some suspicions, but it's nothing major, so don't worry." He pauses. "How are the kids?"

"Jacob's in bed and Autumn's getting a bath before she goes to bed." I turn away just as I hear an extra big splash and wince. "Maybe Wade is getting a bath too. I'm not sure."

Drew chuckles. "Better go check on them then. I'll text you when we're on our way home."

"Thanks. Keep me posted." I end the call and turn to find Autumn's already out of the draining tub, a thick pink towel wrapped around her tiny body. She's grinning up at me, bouncing on her feet.

"Uncle Wade took care of me!" she declares.

My gaze finds Wade's. He's drenched. His T-shirt, his hair, all of him is soaking wet and I try my best to stifle the laughter trying to escape.

"I think Uncle Wade needs a towel too," I say with amusement as I pass him one of those thick towels. Somehow he appears even more masculine drying his hair with a pink towel, his bulging biceps making my knees weak, but I keep that comment to myself.

Autumn's exhausted so it's a breeze putting her to bed. I leave her bedroom to find Wade lingering in the hallway, his T-shirt still clinging to his chest in the most distracting way possible. I try my best to avert my eyes, but it's difficult. The wet fabric clings to every muscle, accentuating all he's got.

And he's got a lot.

"You want to change into a different shirt?" I ask him.

His expression is one of total relief. "If you can dig one up for me, yeah. I can't believe how much she splashed me. I used four extra towels to clean up all the water on the floor."

I make a mental note to put all of those towels in the washing machine later. "There are a few clean T-shirts in the laundry room that belong to Drew. I'm sure they'll fit you."

Wade follows me into the laundry room and I grab a T-shirt off of the folded stack that sits on top of the dryer. "Here you go—" I whirl around, the words sticking in my throat when I witness what's in front of me.

A shirtless Wade—and the reality is even better than what my imagination conjured up earlier.

My mouth goes dry as my gaze roves over all that bared, smooth skin hungrily. *Wow.* He looks like a Greek statue. Like an Adonis. I don't know if I've ever stood so close to such a fine male specimen on display before. My fingertips tingle and I'm tempted to reach out and touch. Stroke and caress and explore and, and, and…

"Here you go." I shove the shirt in his direction, my fingers coming into the briefest contact with his pecs and my knees literally go weak.

Ridiculous.

"Thanks." He takes the shirt from my grip and tugs it over his head, all of that beautiful skin disappearing, just like that.

I'm immediately disappointed.

"You're welcome." My voice comes out squeaky and I clear my throat. "I appreciate the help."

"You did most of the work." He grabs his wet T-shirt off the floor where he left it and drops it into the nearby sink.

"Well, it is my job," I say, my voice laced with sarcasm.

He cracks a smile. "You do it well."

His words almost sound suggestive.

You wish.

I shove my inner mocking voice into the deepest recesses of my brain.

"You want me to stick around until Drew and Fable come home?" he asks, his voice full of concern.

"Oh, I'll be fine." I smile. He should get out of here. Wade Knox is a distraction I absolutely do not need. "Thank you for offering though."

"Are you sure?" He reaches out and brushes his fingers against my upper arm, making my skin tingle. He only wanted to comfort me but instead all I can think is him taking my clothes off. My thoughts are totally out of control. "I don't mind staying."

"You don't have to. Really I'll probably just go to bed after you leave." My cheeks go hot at my saying the word *bed,* which is silly.

"As long as you're okay with being here by yourself." We both start walking until we end up at the front door. He turns to face me. "You can text me if you need anything, all right?"

"But I don't have your number." I frown.

Wade holds out his hand. "Give me your phone."

I enter my passcode and then hand it to him, and he proceeds to tap away at the screen before handing it back to me. "Just added my number to your contacts. Text me so I have your number too."

"Okay." I do as he says, sending him a simple one-word text.

Hey.

He smiles when he gets it, then pockets his phone. "Call me or text me whenever, okay? See ya."

And with that, he's gone.

Wade

I got out of that house as fast as I could, tormented by my lusty thoughts for the Callahan's nanny.

My palms are literally sweating as I grip my steering wheel tight and I try my best to relax my fingers, cracking the knuckles with a quick flex before I settle my hands on the steering wheel once more. My grip is loose, my thoughts are loose, my emotions are all over the place.

Insane. The girl drives me insane and I barely know her. It makes no sense. She's pretty, yeah. I can't deny I find her attractive. She's nice. She's good with the kids, and I shouldn't find that a turn on, but I sort of do. I like her smile. I like the sound of her voice. She smells like fucking heaven and every time I catch a whiff of her fragrance, I want to sniff her all over. See if she smells that good everywhere.

If I don't watch it, I could become a man obsessed.

And that's not good.

Not at all.

chapter
Five

Sydney

Luckily enough Drew and Fable came home just past midnight, and I was still awake, anxiously awaiting their return. Drew had texted me around eleven, letting me know she was going to be released soon and everything was fine. He also told me they were taking an Uber Black back home, so I didn't have to worry about picking them up—considering I offered.

After Drew got Fable settled in bed, he asked me to take care of the kids this morning so Fable could get some extra rest. I readily agreed.

So here I am, taking care of the kids—yeah, that's my job, but usually Fable is always nearby. Jacob is sitting in his highchair eating his breakfast and Autumn is at the table, talking nonstop while she pushes strawberry slices around on her plate with a fork. She's not much of a big eater, which worries Fable. I can tell. Jacob, on the other hand, will shove anything in his mouth you give him.

"Mommy!" Autumn exclaims, and I whirl around to find Fable standing at the entrance of the kitchen, wearing a black robe with the belt cinched tight around her tiny waist. Her hair is disheveled and her eyes are sleepy, but otherwise, she looks completely normal.

"Hey baby," Fable says as Autumn hops off her chair and runs toward her mother. They embrace before Fable hauls her up into her arms and gives her a kiss on the nose. "How'd you sleep?"

"Good! Uncle Wade gave me a bath last night and I splashed him!" Autumn giggles and Fable laughs too.

"Poor Wade." Fable's gaze meets mine. "Thank you for helping with everything. I know it was chaotic, but Drew said you seemed to handle it all like a pro."

Please. I freaked the hell out. Fell down, cried, made a fool of myself. Handled it like a pro? I don't think so. "It was no problem," I say easily.

She sets Autumn back in her chair at the table before she turns to me, her expression suddenly very serious. "There are some things that happened last night though, and I'd like to talk to you about it."

Dread washes over me, slow yet all-consuming. Doesn't help that the dire tone of her voice sets me on edge. "Um, of course."

We walk over to stand by the pantry, where we have enough privacy yet can watch the children as well.

"Are you all right?" I ask before she can say anything. "I

hope you're feeling better."

"Oh yeah. I just had…a moment. They said I had low blood pressure and that's why I fainted." She offers me an embarrassed smile. "I haven't been getting much sleep lately, and I really haven't been eating much either. I need to take care of myself better."

"As long as you're okay." I want her to know that I care about her, because I do. She's not only a great boss, but I also really like her and her family. They've accepted me so easily since I've started, and those first few days, I was a bit of a wreck.

"I'm definitely okay." Fable smiles then glances in the direction of her children, making sure they're all right before she returns her attention to me. "So look. I don't want to freak you out," she starts, promptly freaking me out. "But the media got a hold of some photos of you and Drew from last night and now they're…everywhere."

I frown. This is not the direction I expected her to take this conversation. "Everywhere?"

She nods. "Drew told me about the paparazzi hanging out in front of the restaurant last night, but he blew it off. Said it was no big deal."

"I guess so. I've never dealt with something like that before. I mean, they were asking all kinds of intrusive questions, but I would think that's their normal behavior, right?"

"Yes, that's pretty normal. But they're jumping all over this one particular photo." Fable whips her phone out of her robe pocket and taps on the screen before holding it out for me to see. "Look at this."

The headline above the photo captures me first. It screams

in bold type, *Niner QB Drew Callahan Cradles the Naughty Nanny Close!*

Naughty Nanny? Talk about ridiculous.

My gaze drops to the photo just below the sensationalized headline. It's of Drew, and he's holding me in his arms, my cheek pressed against his chest. He's glaring at the cameras, his expression full of angry irritation and I'm oblivious.

"I fell, when we were trying to get into the SUV," I tell Fable, unable to tear my gaze away from that stupid photo. I guess it does look incriminating, Drew holding me close and the angry expression on his face—we look like we have something to hide. But nothing happened. He just wanted to get to the car so we could pick up Fable and take her to the hospital. "What exactly does the article say?"

"Trust me, you don't want to read the article. You don't want to read any of them. They all say the same thing." Fable shoves her phone back into her pocket. "The media will make up anything to sell a magazine, a photo, a story. It doesn't matter what really happened."

Alarm makes my spine stiffen. Wait a minute. There are *multiple* articles about Drew and me? Talk about surreal. And the tiniest bit frightening. "What are they saying?"

"That you and Drew are involved in a mad, passionate affair and I'm nowhere to be found. I'm a horrible wife and mother who's neglecting my husband's needs, as well as the children's. So that leads him to seek out a much younger woman—the newly hired nanny." Fable rolls her eyes. "So ridiculous."

"Right," I say slowly, studying her. She doesn't look mad, but sometimes you can never tell. My mom is good at that. She can pretend everything's fine, but really she's furious. "You don't believe what they're saying, do you?"

"No, of course not!" She sounds offended by my question. "I know my husband. He would *never* cheat on me."

Whew. Glad she's so firm on that subject. "Well, I have absolutely no interest in your husband whatsoever."

"Oh, I know, Sydney. And I appreciate you saying so." She smiles, but it's strained. "We're hoping we can ignore this and the rumors and speculation will eventually die down. That's what's happened before."

Yikes. This is something they've had to deal with before? How awful. "But what if it doesn't quiet down? What if they keep talking about it? About...Drew and me? What then?"

"Well, Drew has a publicist, and he's pretty savvy. I'm sure he'll help us figure out what to do next." Fable smiles brightly and it almost feels—false. As if she's trying to convince herself everything's going to be just fine. "I'm not too worried, so you shouldn't be either!"

Her casual enthusiasm is almost reassuring, but it feels a little off. What if this bogus story really does become a big deal? When it's a slow news day or week the media tends to grab hold of something and never let it go. They can turn a false rumor into a bigger deal than it was ever supposed to be. I don't want my face splashed all over tabloids and gossip websites.

Talk about embarrassing.

What if my parents find out? I'm almost certain they will. Mom loves to read those gossip sites. And once they find out, they're going to be furious. They don't even know I'm working this nanny job. They'll jump to conclusions first and ask questions later. They've always thought the worst of me, especially my mother. It's their automatic response, when I've never given them reason to doubt me or think I'm some sort of pathetic loser.

But that's how they make me feel—like a loser. The moment they hear about this, they'll probably demand I come home so they can take care of me.

Heaven forbid I learn how to take care of myself. This so-called punishment they're putting me through is supposed to be some sort of test. They want me to cave and come running back to them.

I won't do it. No matter how much bullshit is thrown at me, I won't give in.

I won't let them win.

"Should I say anything?" When Fable frowns, I continue. "To the media. Should I make some sort of statement?"

"No way." Fable shakes her head. "The safest thing to do is ignore it for now. Like I said, most everything you read online and in the tabloids is completely false. You can't trust the media. If you were to talk to them, they'd twist your words around and proclaim you're in love with Drew or something stupid like that. Please don't talk to them."

"Okay," I say with a nod. "I hope...I hope you're not mad at me."

The shock on Fable's face is obvious. "Why would I be mad at you?"

"The photographers last night—we weren't expecting them. It was a total fiasco. But I was so focused on getting the kids out of there, I really didn't pay them that much attention. And then

I fell and it looks like I caused even more problems." My knees are bruised this morning, and a little scraped up, but it's no big deal.

No, the real big deal is the photo, and all the articles about my supposed affair with Drew. I'd always heard that so much of the celebrity gossip is false. Now here's actual proof.

"You're okay after the fall, right?" Fable asks, pushing me out of my thoughts. "Do you need to see a doctor?"

"Oh, I'm fine. Really. Just a little bruised." I shrug.

Fable smiles, though it's faint. She still looks tired. "Thank you so much for taking care of our children last night. Drew and I appreciate it—*you*—more than you'll ever know." She grabs hold of my hand, giving it a light squeeze. "You've gone above and beyond your duties these last few weeks since you've been here. I hate that you've had to go through this, but it'll pass. I know it will."

I smile at her in return, but it doesn't feel real. I hope I haven't upset her. I hope she'll still believe me in a week or two. Or even in five. I don't want to have an affair with her husband. Despite the chemistry between Wade and I last night, I definitely don't want to start anything with him either. A relationship, even a casual one, will be nothing but a distraction at this point in my life.

A distraction I absolutely don't need.

chapter
Six

Sydney

It doesn't pass. A week goes by and it's all the tabloids can talk about. That one same photo is splashed everywhere. Every. Where. In black and white, in full on color, in HD—hell, there's even a video that stupid TMZ somehow got of the two of us fleeing the restaurant with the children, looking like we're together when we are so not. Unfortunately, luck isn't on our side, and nothing big happens in the celebrity world to take their attention off of us.

And when I say us, I mean Drew and…me.

It's ridiculous. There is so much speculation on the various gossip sites and magazines it's embarrassing. I made the freaking cover of *In Touch Weekly*, me and Drew together in that photo where I'm in his arms, front and center on a newsstand in the middle of the supermarket, at the check out lines in Target and Walmart. Everywhere.

I hate it.

My phone has been blowing up with texts, missed calls, voicemail messages and constant notifications. People I haven't talked to since high school are reaching out, asking me if it's true, asking me if I really am having an affair with Drew Callahan.

It's humiliating. My life has turned into a giant mess. It feels like it won't ever stop. I'm afraid I could get fired, even though Fable has reassured me repeatedly that's not going to happen.

Hiding away in my room on my day off is not going to solve any problems. But it's like I can't make myself get out of my big, comfortable bed. I'm starting to wonder if my butt is permanently glued to the mattress. Maybe I'll become bedridden. Housebound. I'll be considered a hermit, a freak, a weirdo, a girl who let one stupid rumor get out of hand and now there's no way she can ever get away from it.

I thought my parents cutting me off was the worst thing that ever happened to me. This situation is even more awful.

A brisk knock sounds on my door and before I can utter, "Go away," because that was what I planned on saying, the door swings open and Fable Callahan enters my bedroom. She stops at the foot of the bed, her expression stern as she watches me wallow in my misery in my messy bed.

From the look on her face alone, I know it's going to be bad. She's going to fire me. I'm sure of it.

"Are you going to stay in bed all day?" she asks, her voice surprisingly firm.

I grab my phone and check the time. 11:52 a.m. "Definitely," I say as I set my phone back on the bedside table.

An irritated sigh leaves her and she comes to my side of

the bed, reaching over to tear the covers off of me completely. "Hey!" I protest, but Fable just takes a step back, hands on her hips as she watches me.

"You need to get up."

"I don't want to." I grab the covers and pull them back over me.

She lifts a brow in surprise. "You sound like Autumn. Next thing you're going to say is I can't make you." Fable tugs the comforter back off of me, tossing it onto the floor. "I know it's your day off and I should probably leave you alone, but enough is enough. You need to get out of bed and get on with your life. Plus, we want to talk to you."

Nerves tangle my stomach, making me queasy. I swallow hard, trying to hide my fear but it's no use. "Is everything okay?" My voice shakes and I briefly close my eyes. Could I sound more pitiful?

"It's nothing bad, I promise." Her voice is soft and soothing and I crack open my eyes to find she's still watching me. "We believe we've come up with a solid plan for handling the media."

"Whose 'we'?"

"Drew and me." Fable grabs hold of my ankle and gives my foot a little shake. "Come on, Sydney. Hear us out. We're excited to tell you about it, but it'll only work with your cooperation. So we hope you'll be on board."

I'm wary. I can't help it. What sort of plan is she talking about? My brother Gabe always used to come up with plans to trick our parents, trick his friends, trick the housekeeper, whatever. He was always coming up with something crazy. A lot of the time, those plans backfired, but he always meant well.

There's a pang in my heart that makes me realize I miss Gabe. A lot. He's called a few times since the bogus story broke. He's texted me, messaged me on Instagram, left me multiple voicemail messages, the works. And I still haven't responded.

I'm too ashamed—and I didn't even do anything wrong. Imagine if I had?

"Why don't you go take a shower and then come downstairs? We can have lunch and discuss our idea."

Sighing, I sit up, pushing the hair out of my face. "Give me forty-five minutes?"

"Perfect." Fable smiles. "See you in a bit."

And with that, she walks out of my room, slowly closing the door behind her.

I grab my phone before I flop back onto the mattress, my head sinking in the pillows as I check my notifications. I ignore most of the texts, especially the one from my mother. She's left me endless messages and voicemails too—the voicemails I've deleted without listening to them. The texts I go ahead and delete as well.

Though I do open up the string of texts from my brother.

Tell me it's not true.

No way are you banging Drew Callahan, are you?

I know you're not that dumb, Syd! Keep your head on straight.

I hear his wife can be mean! She'll kick your ass!

Answer me, Syd. I wanna make sure you're okay.

Syd! Call me! Mom won't stop texting me about you!

Come on, baby sis. Talk to me.

Lucy's worried about you.

We're all worried about you.

There are a few more texts along the same lines, including one that says he loves me, accompanied by a bunch of heart emojis. I can't take it. We're close. We've given each other endless crap over the years, but we always take care of each other too.

Gabe must be really worried.

I decide to go ahead and text him.

I'm fine. I love you too. Miss you.☺

Immediately the gray bubble pops up, indicating Gabe's texting me back.

Call me.

My heart starts to race. Why am I so nervous to talk to him? It's just Gabe. He won't judge. He's done so many stupid things, he can't say squat to me about bad choices. Besides, this ridiculous rumor is just that—a rumor. I'm not having an affair with my boss.

So why am I afraid to talk to Gabe about it? I need to call him. I need to reassure him that everything's okay.

Just as I'm about to dig up his number, my phone rings.

"I thought you were avoiding me," is his greeting.

"I was."

He chuckles, but there's not much humor there. "I've been worried about you."

"I'm fine." I sigh. "It's all just a huge misunderstanding. It's not even true. None of it."

"I figured. What happened?"

I give him all the details, and he lets loose a string of curses after I finish. "Sounds like the media is a bunch of lying sacks of shit."

Leave it to my big brother to be so blunt.

"They are. They won't let the story go either."

"I know. I saw you on the cover of some trashy magazine at the grocery store."

Closing my eyes, I exhale loudly. "It's so embarrassing. What's Mom saying?"

"You don't even want to know."

"Just tell me." God, seriously I don't want to know, but he'd tell me regardless.

"At first, she couldn't believe you even had a job. That's all she could focus on. Then she didn't understand how you got it in the first place, and that you were working for such famous people—direct quote."

"Did you tell her you helped me get the job?"

"No way. I wanted her to think you're fully capable of taking care of yourself." Gabe pauses for a moment. "You are, you know."

I say nothing to that particular statement. I don't feel like I can take care of myself. Instead I end up making a big mess out of everything.

"Is she embarrassed? Is she ready to disown me for life?"

"Funny enough, she doesn't believe any of it."

If I weren't already lying down I probably would've fallen onto the floor at that particular statement. "Are you serious?"

"Oh yeah. She insists you would never do something so

crazy."

"She's right." Now it's my turn to pause. "You believe me, don't you?"

"Hell yeah, I believe you. I know you wouldn't bone your boss. I mean, sure. He's famous and he's good looking or whatever the hell, but you're not crazy, Syd. Not that crazy, at least."

"Gee, thanks." Despite my sarcastic tone, relief floods me at my brother's reassurance. I close my eyes against the tears that suddenly threaten. "I'm so scared they're going to fire me," I whisper.

"Are they mad over what happened?" Now Gabe sounds pissed. "You can't control the media. Neither can they."

"No, no. They're not mad. Not at all. They've been really cool about the entire thing. But still. I'm a nuisance. I'm the Naughty Nanny—that's what one of the gossip blogs called me and they've all started running with it. Can you believe it?" I'm the farthest thing from naughty. I had a few boyfriends in high school, the most serious one my senior year, and yeah, we had sex a few times before we broke up, right as he was about to leave for college.

And I've been single ever since. I haven't even wanted a boyfriend. I've been too busy trying to figure out how to survive to worry about finding a guy.

"Well then, just roll with it. All this gossip will eventually die down, right? It freaking has to. And once it does, they'll forget all about you and your supposed affair with Drew Callahan. The Naughty Nanny will disappear and you can go on with your life," he says.

"It's just so unfair that I'm being dragged through this." I can whine with my brother. He'll let me, but only for a little while. "I'm innocent. Drew's innocent." And they definitely don't want to mention Fable fainting at the restaurant. They want all of us to keep it a secret, and I'm fine with that. Truly, they're lucky no restaurant employees saw it happen.

"Life's unfair sometimes, sis. You just have to learn how to roll with the punches and keep making it happen," Gabe says.

"Okay, Mr. Cliché," I tease him. But then I get serious. "Thank you for talking to me. For supporting me."

"I will always support you. And talk to you. Anytime you need me, don't hesitate to reach out, okay? I love you."

"Love you too." After I end the call, I realize I still need to get ready before I go talk to Drew and Fable.

I grab clothes and head into the connecting bathroom, hurriedly turning on the shower.

Wade

Practice this last week has totally kicked my ass. It's been brutally intense, hours on end of doing drills, catching the ball again. And again. And again. Most of the time, I make it. Sometimes, I miss. Or I drop it. I tripped over my own goddamn feet and went slamming into the ground just this afternoon. A few of the guys laughed at me—I'm sure they were glad it wasn't them—but I picked myself up and shook it off every single time. The more I go out on that field to practice, the more I want to be there. I *need* to be there.

I'm still on the team, too. They haven't cut me yet. There

was a preseason game last Saturday night and I got to play in the last part of the third and all of the fourth quarter. I only caught a single pass but was tackled before I could make it into the end zone.

Not bad for my first official time playing for the 49ers.

The whole Drew and Sydney affair has been the talk of the locker room. They say women like to gossip? Pretty much every locker room I've spent time in over the years has been full of speculation and rumors. They don't talk about the scandal in front of Drew for fear of pissing him off, but they're all whispering about it. Except for me.

I'm the only one who knows the truth.

Drew called me first thing this morning and asked if I'd come over for lunch at their house today. Said he wanted to talk to me about something. I figure it has to do with the team, so of course I said yes. I know some of the other guys are irritated with and jealous of my friendship with Drew. I can't help it that I've known him for so many years, that he practically treats me like family.

And I'm not stupid. I will take advantage of every bit of information Drew feeds me — and he feeds me a lot. He wants to help. I willingly accept that help any and every chance I get.

The moment I enter the Callahan house, though, I realize whatever we're going to talk about has nothing to do with football. Drew takes me to the kitchen, where Autumn is sitting at the counter eating and Fable and Sydney appear to be making lunch. Drew gets us both a beer and hands the bottle over before grabbing his own, snapping off the cap and taking a long drink.

"We need to talk to you," he says after he swallows, his

voice deadly serious, as is his expression.

I'm a little taken aback by his dire tone. And the way he pushed the beer on me. He's not a big drinker, especially before the season starts. And neither am I. I don't bother opening the one he gave me either. I don't want it.

"What about?" I ask warily.

"Oh, don't scare him, Drew." Fable comes to stand beside her husband, a welcoming smile on her face. She looks a lot better compared to the last time I saw her. "We have a— proposition for you."

I glance over at Sydney, who's still standing behind the kitchen counter. She looks as lost as I feel, so I'm guessing she has no idea what they're talking about either. "What sort of proposition?"

"You want to have some lunch first, and then we'll discuss it?" Fable suggests brightly.

"Maybe we should discuss it now." I'm not one for prolonging conversations. When someone tells you, "we need to talk," it's usually bad news. I'd rather get it out right away. No use waiting.

Drew and Fable look at each other before they turn their attention onto me. "Okay, let's talk now then," Drew says easily. "You ready, Sydney?"

"Yeah." Her shaky voice makes me turn and study her closely. Her eyes are wide and unblinking and she looks petrified.

How the hell is she involved in this conversation?

All four of us go to the small table in the breakfast nook. Drew and Fable sit across from Sydney and me, and it almost feels like they're our parents about to rip into us for our bad behavior.

Sounds crazy, I know, but my imagination is wandering.

"We know this is going to sound odd, but please hear us out," Fable starts. "We came up with an idea to distract the media, and it involves both of you."

We both say nothing and Fable takes that as her cue to keep talking.

"Everyone keeps talking about Drew and the 'Naughty Nanny'. " She even adds air quotes. "Now, the four of us know the stories aren't true. We were there that night, and we all know what really happened. We want to keep the fainting incident out of the public eye, because first, it's no one's business what happens to me, and second..." Her voice drifts and her eyes start to shine. Like she might burst into tears at any moment.

Ah, hell. I hope she's not going to give us bad news.

Drew rests his hand over his wife's before he turns his attention to us and says, "Fable is pregnant again. Her doctor thinks that's why she fainted."

Wow. Another baby. That's unexpected. "But this is good news, right?" I watch them carefully, noting the worry in both of their gazes.

"It's great news," Drew says as he looks over at Fable. "We're thrilled. But Fable's pregnancy with Jacob wasn't the easiest, especially near the end. She had some minor problems and her doctor warned her they could become worse if she gets pregnant again. She's going to need to take it easy with this pregnancy. We don't want her to end up on bed rest. Or worse, in the hospital."

"So how do we come into this? How can we help?" Sydney asks, her eyes wide. She seems a little stunned at the pregnancy announcement so I'm figuring she didn't know.

"Well, Fable is going to take it easy these next couple of weeks and stay close to home. And while we appreciate all that you do—"

Sydney doesn't even let Drew finish his sentence. "You're firing me, aren't you." She's not asking, she's stating what she thinks is the obvious. Then she lays her head down on the table, burying her face against her arms.

If she starts crying, I'm going to lose it.

"We're not firing you," Fable says, her voice gentle. "I definitely need you around, especially right now. But I have another task for you as well."

"What sort of task?" Sydney's voice is muffled by her arms since she won't lift her head.

"We want you to pretend to be Wade's girlfriend," Fable says, her gaze cutting to mine.

Say freaking *what?*

chapter Seven

Wade

Sydney lifts her head, her expression incredulous. "You want me to pretend to be Wade's *girlfriend? Why?"*

Damn. Why does she sound so offended? I don't think I'm the shit, but come on. I'm okay looking, an NFL team drafted me, and if all goes well, I'll have a solid income for the next five to ten years that could set me up for life.

I'm not a bad catch, especially if you're just playing pretend. So what's her deal?

"It would be a great distraction for the media," Drew explains, his gaze locked on Sydney. "They'd forget all about me and you and how we're supposedly having this wild affair. They could focus on your relationship with the new wide receiver for the Niners instead, right? We could even possibly make a special announcement—"

Fable interrupts him. "No. A special announcement is a

terrible idea. They'll just twist our words around and make us look even guiltier."

Fable's right. I totally agree. So I decide to speak up.

"You don't think the media will be suspicious that we've made up a *fake* relationship to cover up your supposed affair with Sydney?" When Drew directs his thunderous expression toward me, I throw up my hands. "I'm not saying the affair is true. I know it's not true. But I'm talking about the public perception. Will our newfound relationship look like some sort of publicity stunt to take the focus off of you and Sydney together?"

"It won't look like a publicity stunt if you two really play up the fact that you're crazy about each other," Fable points out.

I look over at Sydney, whose cheeks are turning a bright pink. She's embarrassed. She's probably not down for this idea at all, despite all that attraction we had buzzing between us a few nights ago. And hey, when I take my personal feelings out of it, I understand. Why should she agree? Why should I? What do we gain out of this? Absolutely nothing. What they're proposing is insane.

Yet despite the insanity, I'm still intrigued.

"I know this sounds ridiculous, but hear us out." Drew leans forward, resting his forearms on the table. "The media is on a total rampage in search of a scandalous story. They've targeted me, and they've targeted Sydney, and they act like they never want to let our supposed affair go. So let's give them an entirely different story. Let's manipulate the situation so it looks like the two of you are together."

"But how do we convince people we're together?" I ask.

"And who really gives a crap if we are?"

"The paparazzi are after Sydney still. But if they constantly see her with you instead, they'll eventually give up talking about the Naughty Nanny affair story and move on. And we need them to move on." He meets Fable's gaze for a quick moment, his expression softening before he returns his attention to us. "So go out together. Be seen together in public places, at restaurants or wherever you want. Have Sydney over at your place. Have her come to the game this Saturday so she can root for you and look like the perfect girlfriend."

"It might look like she's there to root for you," I point out. I'm not trying to be argumentative. I just want them to see all the possibilities.

"Not if you make a big production about her being there. Giving them no doubt that she's at the game to support you." Drew shakes his head, appearing frustrated. "Look, just trust us. This idea can work. A fake relationship is a great distraction. We know it is."

Come on. How would they know?

I glance over at Sydney, but she's not saying a word. Her lips are thin, like she's pressing them together so tightly they're eventually going to disappear. She looks as uncomfortable as I feel.

What Drew and Fable are proposing is totally insane.

"If we were to agree…" And no, I'm not agreeing. Not yet. "How long do you expect us to keep this up?"

"All we ask for is a week. That's it," Fable says with a nervous smile. "We think a solid seven days will help distract the gossips and get them to focus on something—or someone else."

"Or we'll just fuel their fire and have them questioning everything we do," Sydney points out, her voice trembling.

Her statement is the only logical one in this sea of crazy. What Drew and Fable are proposing is nuts. I don't have time for a relationship, fake or real. I'm trying to put my all into football, into the team, into my teammates. This is a distraction I don't need, because I know spending one-on-one time with Sydney would distract me.

And the scariest part of it all is I wouldn't mind letting her distract me either.

"Please, Wade." Fable turns her big green eyes on me, her voice tremulous. "We need your help, and we thought this was the safest, easiest solution. We know this is a big favor that we're asking of the both of you, and normally we would never propose this type of thing, but all this constant talk of the affair could be damaging Sydney's reputation, and that's not fair. She got drawn into this mess because she works for us. She never asked for any of this." Fable directs her gaze to Sydney. "We're so sorry, Sydney. I wish we could make all of this disappear."

"It's not your fault," Sydney says softly, her head bent, dark blonde hair falling into her face. "I don't blame you or Drew."

Fable's gaze meets mine. "It's not only Sydney's reputation that's being harmed, it's Drew's too. And mine. Our entire family's reputation is at stake, especially now that I'm pregnant."

She has a point. The paparazzi would speculate endlessly over her pregnancy, the supposed affair with the nanny...

"We don't want Drew to lose his endorsements, all over a false story. And maybe with you gaining a little attention from this fake relationship could help with endorsements for you in the future. You never know." Fable tries to smile but fails, so she gives up.

And man, if that doesn't make me feel like shit.

"So what you're telling us is that you want to create another false story to counter all the negativity that's fallen upon you and Drew," I point out, stating the obvious. I don't mean to be an asshole, but that's exactly what they're doing. Lies upon lies don't necessarily solve the problem.

I've learned that a few times in my life.

Fable actually looks hurt and I immediately regret what I've said. "When you put it like that, you make us sound awful, but that's not our intent. We want to help Sydney. And we need help too."

"I hate asking this of you, but it's only a week. That's not very long," Drew adds. "Think about it."

I turn to look at Sydney, who's studying me with a wary gaze. "Want to go outside and talk about this?"

She doesn't say a word. She doesn't need to. Instead, she rises to her feet and we both head for the backyard.

The moment I shut the door behind us, Sydney's pacing the length of the patio, scowling at the ground as she starts talking.

"This is the craziest idea I've ever heard. Seriously. And I've heard some crazy crap in my life. My brother is always coming up with outrageous schemes, ever since he was a little kid. But they want us to be in a fake relationship? I mean…really? That's ridiculous. You don't want to be with me, and I sure as hell don't want to be with you."

Ouch. "Tell me how you really feel," I drawl, crossing my arms. Guess she doesn't like me much after all.

Sydney comes to a sudden stop. At least she looks embarrassed by what she said. "I'm sorry. Really. I wasn't trying to be mean. It's just…"

"You have no desire to be with me. I get it." I drop my arms to my sides and tell myself to get over my hurt feelings. "Let's consider the situation, though. We need to be realistic."

"Okay."

"You need this fake relationship way more than I do."

"I've been dealing with the situation as best I can," she mutters, sounding irritated.

"How? By hiding out in the Callahan mansion and pretending those stories out there don't exist?" By the way she flinches, I'm guessing I just nailed her recent behavior pretty accurately. "You've made the front page of a few gossip rags. I saw you on the cover of some magazine at the supermarket."

"You go to the supermarket?"

I roll my eyes. "I have to eat, right?" If she thinks I'm some sort of superstar like Drew who's mobbed any time I set foot out in public, she's completely off base. "Despite your hiding, the stories aren't going away. Maybe pretending to be something that we're not is the right thing to do."

Sydney nods, like she gets what I'm saying. But I don't even know if she's able to focus on the words that just came out of my mouth. I think she's too wrapped up in her own turbulent thoughts.

"This will pass," she says firmly. "The reporters or whoever they are will all move on when some other star does something crazy. Maybe Tom Brady and Giselle will finally get a divorce. Who knows? But the media can't hold onto this story forever, especially when there's nothing real behind it." Her confident words are belied by that slight tremble in her voice. She's nervous. Maybe she doesn't believe this story is going to fade anytime soon, and Drew and Fable don't believe it will either.

That's why they want Sydney and me to pretend we're in a relationship. That she's my girlfriend and I'm her boyfriend and she belongs to me. I've been a player. I've messed around with many a girl over the years, but never once have I had a steady girlfriend. For the longest time, I firmly believed I didn't need one. Once Owen got together with Chelsea, and I saw what a great relationship they shared, I knew someday I would want something like what they have.

Just not yet.

Tilting my head to the side, I study Sydney. Really study her for the first time, and I have to admit...

I like what I see. She's pretty. Average height and a bangin' body from what I can tell, with striking blue eyes and wavy golden blonde hair and that kissable mouth. There's no denying we have chemistry. I've felt it. I'm feeling it right now.

Hell. I scrub a hand over my face, telling myself I shouldn't focus on just how kissable her mouth is. If we really do this, I wonder how far I'll have to take this fake relationship thing. Will we hold hands? Will I have to slip my arm around her shoulders, her waist? Will we kiss in public? That might get weird.

Or then again, it might not...

Sydney

Wade is blatantly checking me out. And when I say blatantly, I also mean thoroughly. Like I can feel his gaze scan the length of my body, lingering on certain parts. My face. My chest. My legs.

The typical guy checking out a girl deal.

So I decide to give him a taste of his own medicine. I check him out right back, starting at the top of his dark, shaggy hair and cruising on down. But he has more body to check out, only because he's so much bigger than me. His shoulders are broad, as is his chest, and his arms are thick with muscle. He has a trim waist and hips, big thighs...he's a big man. With a beautiful face. Dark brown eyes and a sharp nose and high cheekbones and that jawline...I'm a sucker for a good jawline. There's something so inherently male, so sexy about a strong jaw to me.

And Wade has one of the best jawlines I've ever seen.

He has full lips. Nice, straight teeth.

"Do I measure up?" he asks, his voice full of amusement.

"Do I?" I throw back at him with a glare.

"Touché." He smiles and my glare disappears. Wade has a nice smile too. He has a nice everything, truth be told.

But do I really want to pretend I'm in a relationship with him for a week? A week's a long time. A lot of things could happen. This could also be a pointless endeavor. The reporters and gossip people might not believe us. They're not dumb. They'll probably see right through our plan. How are we supposed to act like a real couple anyway? Throw ourselves at each other?

Kiss each other, hang all over each other? We might not have any chemistry...

Oh, I'm in total denial. We definitely have chemistry. I feel a buzz when we're in the same room together, let alone when we're alone or when he actually touches me.

It wouldn't be a total hardship, pretending Wade Knox is my boyfriend.

"You want me to be honest? I think the idea's crazy," Wade says, interrupting my thoughts. "But Drew and Fable have done so much for me over the years. I almost feel like I owe them. I mean, how bad can it be, letting photographers see us together for a few nights in a row? We can hold hands, shoot each other longing looks, and hopefully that'll end all the Drew-with-the-nanny speculation that's currently going on."

"Do you really think it's going to help?" He frowns at me, and I continue. "Us pretending we're a couple. I mean, can we make the two of us together seem believable?"

Wade shrugs those impossibly broad shoulders of his. "It can't hurt to give it a try. Unless you have a problem with spending time with me."

"I don't have a problem spending time with you," I say hurriedly, making him smile.

But I can't smile in return. My mind is a whirl of emotions. This is crazy. Insane. I shouldn't agree. I barely know this guy. Truly, I barely know the people asking me to do this either. What if Drew and Fable are a bunch of weird psychos who get their kicks torturing other people just for their amusement?

It could happen. Run with me here.

"So. Are you in?" Wade asks, his deep, rumbly voice

breaking through my thoughts.

How have I never noticed just how sexy his voice is before?

"Are you?" I ask with a raised brow.

Another shrug. "Yeah. I think I am."

"Before I commit, I need to know a few things about you first." I grab a patio chair and sit down, then wave at him to do the same.

He chooses the one directly across from me, of course. Settling that big body of his into the chair, his thighs spread wide in that typical guy way, he studies me. "What do you want to know?"

"Where are you from?"

"I grew up in Chico. Went to college there too."

"Ah." I nod. "Brothers or sisters?"

"None. Only child." His mouth goes thin. "Single mom."

Aw. "I'm sure she's really proud of you and all that you've accomplished," I say softly.

"She is. That's why I'm working so damn hard to stay on the team. I don't want to disappoint her."

"But I thought you were already on the team?" I'm so confused.

"I am, but they can still cut me. If I'm still there after the last preseason game, I'm pretty much in."

I'm sort of clueless when it comes to sports. I've never had an athletic boyfriend before. I was always drawn more to the soulful musician types. The tall, lanky boys who wrote bad poetry and thought they could change the world with a song.

Yeah. Wade Knox is nothing like those types of guys.

"Oh. Well, I'm sure you'll remain on the team." I sound

confident, but really, I have no clue. "What was your major in college?"

"Finance. I wanted to make sure I knew how to properly manage money and investments, especially if I was going into the NFL."

Well, I have to admire his drive. He's planning his future and not just counting on football, which is smart.

"Gotcha," I say with a nod. *Gotcha?* Really? I sound ridiculous. "And your best friend is Fable's brother?"

"Yep. Owen Maguire. He just got drafted by the Broncos."

My mouth drops open, but then I snap it shut. I somehow forgot Fable told me about her brother, the newly drafted Denver Bronco. Seriously, what is up with all of these football players? It's downright surreal. "Are you serious?"

"Uh huh. He's a great player. He's the one who wanted to get picked up by the Niners so he can stay close to his family." Guilt crosses his face but it's gone in an instant. "Instead, I'm the one who's with the Niners and playing with his brother-in-law."

He feels bad about that, I can tell. And it's kind of sweet.

"Is the job interview finished?" Wade asks amusedly.

I smile. "I think so."

"Am I worthy?"

I tap my index finger against my chin as I watch him. "Still contemplating."

"Well, while you're contemplating, it's my turn to ask you a few questions." He clears his throat as he leans forward, his hands linked in front of him. He looks very serious, like he really is about to interview me. "Where did you grow up?"

"Texas. Here in California. Everywhere."

Wade raises a brow. "You traveled a lot?"

"Sort of." I don't want to tell him too much. I don't want the poor little rich girl judgment. Not that I think Wade would be judgey, but I don't know. People treat you differently when they realize you come from wealth.

"Brothers or sisters?" He's totally copying my earlier line of questions.

"An older brother. Gabe. My parents are still together, but we think they hate each other."

"That sucks," he murmurs with a slight shake of his head. "You're nineteen, right?"

"Yes." Unease trickles down my spine. What else could he ask me? I have a few secrets, and I'm not big on revealing them, especially to a stranger. Even Drew and Fable don't know everything about me. How I ended up with this job is kind of embarrassing.

As in, everyone was doing me a favor.

"Do you go to college?"

I look away from him, my brain scrambling to come up with an excuse. "I'm saving up for college right now. I can't really afford it." I meet his gaze once more, trying to appear confident. More like I didn't go, I lied to my parents that I was, and that lie ruined everything.

And there's no one else I can blame but myself.

"I understand that. Luckily enough, I got a football scholarship."

"You must be really good."

Yet another shrug. "I'm all right."

He's so modest too. This guy is almost too good to be true.

"We should do this. We should help them," I tell him before I chicken out. "We've got nothing to lose. How hard can it be?"

"So I guess I passed the test?" He smiles and the sight of it makes my heart race.

He is really too good-looking. I don't know how I'm going to spend time with him and act like a normal human being. Of course, maybe it's good that I won't act normal. I'll be a starry-eyed dork instead. Maybe that'll be more convincing.

"Did I pass *your* test?" I ask him.

The appreciative glow in his eyes as he studies me is obvious. And it makes me warm. "Oh yeah."

"Okay then." I take a deep breath and stand, resting my hands on my hips. "Let's go inside and tell them we're going to go through with this."

chapter Eight

Sydney

I seriously cannot believe we're going to do this.

Wade and I have spent the last week going over stuff, collaborating our stories, making up our newly formed, shared background. Well, more like Fable and I have been putting this stuff together while Drew and Wade are at intensive practices, and then I share the info with Wade via text or when he comes over to the house. For days now Fable and I have been spending time with the kids and creating my make-believe relationship with Wade. In the evening, I talk with Wade, letting him know what we've come up with. He just nods and agrees, never protesting, but never offering his opinion either.

I think he's distracted by practice, by the upcoming game. It's the last preseason game and he's playing. Deep down, I think he's petrified he'll get kicked off the team. This is the final make-or-break moment for him, and he's nervous. Edgy. So I do my best to talk to him and soothe his jangled nerves.

I don't know if it's working or not, but at least I'm trying.

It's been kind of fun, making up this entire dream-like relationship between Wade and me. How we met each other the day Fable hired me (truth) and it was love at first sight. We've been seeing each other ever since (truth—as in we do literally see each other quite often since he comes over to the Callahan house all the time). So it's not like we're lying...

But then again, we so are. Everything about this situation is fake. I mean, yeah, I think Wade is attractive. I'm guessing he finds me attractive too. But can we really pull this off? Can we really convince the media—the world—that we're madly in love and only have eyes for each other?

I don't know.

We decided against Fable or Drew doing any sort of formal announcement. It felt too forced and we were afraid the media wouldn't buy it.

Honestly? I still worry they won't buy what we're trying to sell them. A relationship with Wade looks awfully convenient, doesn't it? I'm fully prepared for the media to ask me a lot of questions. And I think my answer to most of them is going to be...

No comment.

"What was Wade like when he was younger?" I ask Fable while we're hanging out in the kids' playroom upstairs on Friday afternoon. Jacob is toddling around picking up plastic blocks and throwing them back down onto the ground. Autumn is sitting at a tiny table with a coloring book open and a box of crayons spilled all around her, coloring as if her life depended on it. The grim determination on the girl's face almost makes me want to laugh.

Fable smiles and slowly shakes her head. "He was sort of a nightmare. They both were, Owen and Wade. They'd get in trouble all the time. They made me crazy, but Wade's mom was so good to both of them, and to me. I'm so thankful she helped me out back then. It was a rough time. And those boys just didn't give a shit." She makes a face. "Pardon my language. I've gotten better about the cursing thing, but the occasional bomb flies out."

"Wade was a troublemaker?" I'm surprised. At Fable's questioning look, I continue. "He just seems so…intense all the time. Like he's always trying to do the right thing."

"He's changed a lot these last few years. He's straightened up, gotten serious about his career and what he wants out of life. But there's still a mischievous side to him—a naughty side. I bet it's just buried deep."

Interesting. I wouldn't describe Wade as mischievous. Or naughty. Then again, I don't know him that well at all.

"In college he was a total ladies' man. So was my brother, until he met his girlfriend. She changed his player ways," Fable says.

"Did Wade have a lot of girlfriends?"

Fable shakes her head. "He had a lot of girls, but none of them were serious. I'm telling you, they lived in a well-known party house. Wade always had some girl on his arm, sometimes two, but they never meant anything to him."

Sometimes *two?* "Oh." I understand why he would be a player. I mean, look at him. But I'd never peg him as one now, what with the way he acts most of the time. He seems like the type to keep to himself.

But maybe I've read him totally wrong. I don't have a ton of experience with guys. He could have me totally snowed, and I'd never be the wiser.

"Our lives were so different then." Fable's expression grows distant. "I didn't have the best mother. My dad was nonexistent, and our mom had a drinking problem, so I had to take care of Owen a lot on my own when I was growing up. I became like a second mom to him."

I had no idea. She seems to live this enchanted life. I can't imagine her suffering and having to take care of her brother on her own. "Are you still in contact with your mom?"

"She died a few years ago." Fable sighs. "I sound awful, but it was probably…for the best. She was a drug addict and an alcoholic, and she could never keep a job. Her life was miserable, and she made everyone else around her miserable too."

"I'm sorry." I don't know what else to say. I thought my parents were bad. Her mom sounds awful.

"It's okay. I met Drew and he eventually changed my life for the better." Fable smiles, her expression soft now, and full of happiness. "Maybe it could work out between you and Wade like it did for Drew and me."

"Ah, I don't know about that." I'm suddenly flustered. It's ridiculous to think Wade and I could have something real, something beautiful and full of love like what Drew and Fable share.

"Don't count it out," Fable says, almost cryptically. "He's a good guy. Solid. Smart. Attractive. On the offensive line for the

San Francisco 49ers." She starts to laugh. "You could do worse, you know."

I giggle along with her, shaking my head. "Can I confess something to you?"

Fable's eyes light up. "Of course."

"I don't know anything about football."

The disappointment on Fable's face is clear. "Damn it, I was hoping you were going to tell me something juicy! Like you're already madly in love with Wade and praying he feels the same way."

I can feel my cheeks go hot. "No, I'm not in love with him! Besides, I already told you, I barely know him. This entire situation is all kinds of awkward. I'm terrified we won't be able to pull it off."

"Just go with it," Fable says, her voice firm. "You'll be fine. Your first public outing is tonight, right?"

"Yeah, he's coming back here with Drew." And I'm nervous as hell every time I even think about what we're going to do. I hold up my hands in front of me to see that they're shaking. "I hope I don't make a mess of it."

"You can't make a mess of it if you just be yourself," Fable reassures me.

"That's the part where I think I'll mess it up," I say, making Fable laugh and shake her head.

Jacob chooses that particular moment to walk up to me and throw his yellow plastic block right at my head. I dodge it so the block only grazes my hair and doesn't make actual contact. "Ouch, buddy!"

"Aw, you little meanie." Fable grabs hold of Jacob by the

waist and hauls him into her lap, giving him a little shake and making him laugh. "No throwing blocks at girls!"

"Isn't that the way boys used to show their love?" I tease.

"Yeah, back in kindergarten." Fable tickles Jacob, sending him into peals of laughter. He's so stinking cute. He looks just like Drew, where Autumn resembles Fable, with the exception of her dark hair versus Fable's blonde. "Want me to help you get ready tonight?"

"Would you?"

"Absolutely. We might have these monkeys underfoot, but it shouldn't be too bad."

"I'll take you up on that offer."

"Good." Fable's smile slowly fades. "After all, I'm responsible for you having to deal with all of this. The least I can do is help you as much as possible."

"I don't mind doing it. Spending time with Wade Knox and pretending he's my boyfriend won't be a hardship." Ha, maybe I shouldn't have confessed that.

But hey, I'm being totally honest. It won't be difficult, pretending to be Wade's girlfriend. He's nice, he's attractive, he's a total catch.

"Right?" She holds up her hand, palm out, and I give her a high five. "I think you two are going to be a very convincing couple," Fable says with a big smile.

From her mouth to God's ears, I swear.

Wade

"Ready to do this?" I ask Sydney as she steps out onto the

front porch, shutting the door behind her.

She offers me a nervous smile, running a hand over her blonde hair. How do I know that smile is nervous? Her lips quiver at the corners, I swear. "Ready as I'll ever be," she murmurs.

I take her hand and lead her over to my truck, hitting the keyless remote to unlock the passenger side door. I got ready for our first "date" in the locker room after a particularly intense practice. Once I showered and changed into black pants and a white button down shirt with the sleeves rolled up, I drove over to Drew and Fable's house to pick Sydney up. I'm taking her to a restaurant Fable recommended would be a good one to be seen at. Meaning the paparazzi hang around this specific restaurant all the time.

"You don't have to hold my hand," she says as we come to a stop by the passenger side of my truck.

I let go of said hand to open the door for her. "I'm in practice mode. We need to get used to it. Besides, photographers have been hanging around here lately, right?" I watch as she climbs into my truck. She's wearing a dark blue dress that somehow covers a lot of her, yet shows off plenty of skin too. While I've always believed I was a tit man, I can admit I definitely admire her long, sleek legs.

"Right. They might be lurking outside the gate at this very moment," she says as she pulls the door shut before I can say anything else.

Huh. Seems that someone is more nervous than I thought.

When I pull out of the gate, I notice a single nondescript car parked across the street, and a single guy sitting behind the steering wheel. I'm guessing he's a photographer.

Good. We'll put on a show. Give them what they want.

We drive into the city, making small talk as I navigate our way to the restaurant. Considering it's a Friday night, the traffic is heavy, the streets backed up as we slow to a crawl the closer we get to downtown. The fading sunlight flashes within the truck's cab as we drive, every once in a while, enveloping Sydney in a golden glow. I keep stealing glances in her direction, reminding myself this is only one night, and that everything we're about to embark on, is fake. She feels nothing for me. I'm supposed to feel nothing for her.

Nothing.

Nothing.

Nothing.

We finally arrive at the restaurant fifteen minutes later than the reservation time I made, and I hope like hell we didn't lose our table. I leave my keys with the valet and escort Sydney into the restaurant, clutching her hand once more as we walk inside. She curls her fingers tightly around mine and I glance down, noticing how my hand completely engulfs hers. She's actually pretty tiny. And I'm the complete opposite of that.

"Does this feel weird or what?" Sydney asks after the hostess seats us at our table in the middle of the restaurant.

I glance up from the giant menu the hostess handed us. "Does what feel weird?"

"The two of us. Together." She sends me a pointed look. "Can I confess something?"

"Absolutely." I sit up straighter, my attention focused only on her.

"You're not my usual type." Her gaze drops to the table, her cheeks turning the faintest shade of pink.

The shy act is something I'm not usually attracted to. I like my women bold. I like it when they know what they want. But then again, Sydney isn't my woman. She's not even someone I'm interested in making my woman. I'm pretending to be interested to help some friends out. That's it. I need to remember that.

"You're not my type either," I admit.

Her head jerks up, her wide gaze meeting mine. She looks offended, which is hilarious because she's the one who started this conversation. "What's your type then?"

"You really want to discuss this before dinner?"

Sydney nods. "Oh, I definitely want to discuss this before dinner."

Great. I was ravenous not thirty seconds ago, and now my appetite is evaporating. "We're pretending, so why does it matter what my type is?"

"It matters. We need to act like we're attracted to each other, right? So what type of girl are you attracted to?"

How am I supposed to describe my ideal girl and not sound like a complete jackass?

"How about this," she starts when I still haven't said anything. "I prefer soulful types. Guys who like music so much they want to write it. My past boyfriends have been tall, thin, and they like to play guitar. Oh, and they usually have a piercing or two."

"Who says I don't have a piercing or two?"

Her mouth falls open, those cheeks turning even pinker.

She looks shocked. Good. "Do you?"

I shrug. "You'll never know, will you? Since this is all fake?"

She snaps her mouth shut, struggling to regain her composure. "Shouldn't I know if you have piercings or not? Since I'm your supposed girlfriend?"

"Why? Who's going to ask a question like that?"

"I don't know, but someone could. And I'll look like an idiot if I don't know the answer to that question, especially since we're supposed to have been — intimate with each other."

"We could be like Russell Wilson and his new wife. Claim that we're celibate until we get married. Reporters will eat that up." I have my own feelings about Russell Wilson, but I won't declare them out loud.

"*Married?*" All the air seems to have left her at my words. I think she might've even gasped. "That's a little serious, don't you think?"

"When the relationship is as fake as ours is, you can be as extreme as you want to be." We're already in this deep. What's a little talk about marriage? Women usually love that sort of thing, though I should watch myself. I don't want Sydney to get any ideas.

"Marriage is pretty extreme. Like, the most extreme that you can be." She shakes her head. "Honestly? I'm not a believer. Marriage is more like a trap."

I'm taken aback by her trap comment. She mentioned her parents' marriage was pretty crappy. So maybe she's thinking of that? If that's all she's ever seen, then yeah I can see why she wouldn't believe in marriage. Hell, I'm not a big believer either. My sperm donor didn't even bother marrying my mom.

He knocked her up, stuck around until I was born and then jammed. Never to be seen or heard from again. "I only used it as an example," I say, but she's not even listening to me. She just keeps talking about it.

"I'm only nineteen. The last thing I want to be is *married*." She practically spits out the last word, like it was something disgusting she ate.

"Same. I'm only twenty-two. My life is really just beginning."

"So is mine."

"Well, I guess we're in agreement that we're not ready to get married then." I grin. This conversation — like our situation — is totally insane. "Did we just have our first fight, Sydney?"

"I think so. And we've already resolved it and everything." She returns the smile, her gaze dropping to the menu in front of her. "Maybe it's a good thing I'm changing up my usual type."

"It's always smart to stretch and expand your horizons," I say as seriously as possible.

And maybe I'm starting to believe that too.

chapter
Nine

Sydney

The candlelight from the votive on our table strikes Wade in the most perfect way possible. The flame constantly flickers, casting his face in various shadows that only highlight his features. The more I stare at him throughout our very intimate yet totally on-display dinner, the more I like what I see.

Ugh. I need some sort of warning alarm in my head to remind me what I'm doing is dangerous. Playing around like I'm in a relationship with Wade Knox is stupid. Maybe I was a fool to agree to this.

Too late to reconsider, though—I'm all in, whether I like it or not.

I've felt people watching us all night, and I hope they don't recognize me. But then again, I'm supposed to want them to recognize me. The Naughty Nanny—that nickname is the freaking worst, I swear. I don't want people to believe I'm the one who's possibly breaking up the Callahan marriage.

Hence all this phony stuff, which feels surprisingly real right now—scary, I know. But I can't help it. Wade is so nice, and nice to look at too. I've seen more than one woman stare at him as she passed by our table. I can't blame them either. He's so good looking. I don't even think he knows just how attractive he is.

That makes it even worse.

"People keep looking over at us," Wade says, his voice low as he quickly scans the room. I idly wonder if he's a mind reader. "Think they recognize you?"

"I hope not," I immediately say in return. "Maybe they recognize you."

He scoffs. How he can make a scoff sound sexy, I'm not sure, but he just did. "No way. No one knows who I am, nor do they care."

I like how he just used the word "nor". Crap, I'm liking everything he's doing tonight. I need that danger warning alarm sounding off, stat. "They'll figure out who you are soon when you start playing in the regular season."

He looks pleased by my comment, and I'm proud of the fact that I'm retaining so much of what Fable's taught me about football over this last week. She told me she didn't know squat about the game either when she first started dating Drew, but she wanted to know because it was such a big part of his life.

I'm only learning so I don't sound like an idiot in case anyone asks me about my so-called boyfriend's career, which isn't quite the same as Fable's intentions. But whatever. She knows a lot, she's gone over the basics for me, so I'm fairly confident I won't end up sounding like a complete imbecile if a reporter or whoever asks me about my "boyfriend" and what he does.

"I just want to stay on the team. That's all." Wade sets his fork on his now-empty plate. The man can put a lot of food away, though I guess I shouldn't be surprised considering how large he is. "Tomorrow's game is everything. I have to give it my best."

Right. This game is the most important of his life. He's reiterated that to me more than once. "We should probably leave early so you can get home and get some rest."

"The game isn't until tomorrow night, and besides, I won't be able to sleep." He smiles ruefully. "Too nervous."

It's ridiculous, but I find his nervousness super cute right now. "You'll be fine. You've made it this far. How can it go wrong?"

"Trust me, it can go wrong. It's pretty hard not to think my life has turned into some sort of dream. Since I was seven and in youth league football, I've wanted this. A chance at the NFL, a chance to play football for one of the greatest teams ever. It never seemed possible before, you know? Just one unattainable dream to add to the long list of dreams I had when I was a kid. Something I can chase after, yet never seem to catch." He shrugs, looking embarrassed he just spilled his guts.

But I'm stuck on one minor fact. "You've played football since you were seven?"

"Yeah. My mom put me in peewee football so that it would give me some discipline."

"Did it help?"

"Oh yeah. Well, it gave me an outlet for all my energy and anger too." He takes a sip of his water. "I was kind of a pissed off kid."

"Really? Why?" It's nice sitting here, getting to know him. I don't want to share too many intimate details with him about my background, but I like hearing his stories. Makes me feel closer to him.

"The thing with my dad, how he was never a part of my life. That made me angry, and there was nothing my mom could do about it, so she put me in football. In the hopes it would allow me to channel my energy in a more positive way." He laughs. "She'd be real proud. I sound just like her right now."

"You two are really close, aren't you?" I find that so sweet. Most of the guys I've known would never admit they were close to their parents.

"Yeah. She's all I've got. And I'm all she's got. It's always been the two of us against the world."

"She never remarried?"

"My dad didn't marry her in the first place. But no, she never married. Said she never met a man worthy enough, and she didn't want to bother hooking herself up to a loser just because." His gaze meets mine, dark and intense. "You said you're not a believer in marriage? Well, neither am I. I'm not much of a big believer in true love either. It all sounds like a bunch of shit if you ask me."

"I totally agree," I murmur, my gaze never leaving his. It's like we're bonding over our mutual distaste for love and relationships. While we sit here pretending we're in love and in a relationship.

The irony isn't lost on me. I bet it's not lost on him either.

"No wonder we both so readily agreed to pretend we're in a relationship like this," he says. "We're not believers."

"Not believers of what exactly?" I know what he means, I just want to hear him say it.

"Believers in love." His smile is slow, his gaze still intense. I'm starting to realize that's an apt description of him. He can smile so easily but still appear so serious. Maybe Fable's right — there still might be a hint of mischievousness lingering deep inside him. And I wouldn't mind trying to bring that to the surface. "Love is a total waste of time."

"Totally."

"If you think you've fallen in love, you'll only get hurt."

"Most likely."

"And who wants to get hurt?"

"Definitely not me," I agree.

"Attraction is for real, though."

I frown. His comment just tripped me up. "Attraction?"

"Yeah, you know. Attraction. Chemistry. Being drawn toward someone, and that person being drawn toward you. That's real."

"So you believe in attraction, but not love."

"Of course I believe in attraction. It's what makes the world go 'round. It's what draws people to each other in the first place, and makes them think they're in love." He takes another sip of his water and I watch him, entranced with the way his lips curve around the glass, how his Adam's apple moves when he swallows. Ugh. All this talk of attraction and love is starting to get to me. Just watching him drink is making me squirm, which is totally ridiculous.

"I guess I didn't think you'd be a big believer in attraction. I don't know why," I say, my gaze lingering on his now damp lips. His very full, shiny lips. Is it suddenly hot in here, or is it just me?

"Just because I don't believe in love doesn't mean I won't indulge every once in a while." He chuckles. "I used to indulge a lot more when I was younger."

"With girls?"

"Well, yeah." His cheeks actually turn ruddy, like he's embarrassed. "Most of my college years, you could've totally called me a man-whore and I wouldn't have argued. I was with a different girl every night, it felt like."

I frown. "And why exactly are you telling me this?" Not like college was that long ago for him. For all I know he could've considered himself a man-whore up to a few weeks ago.

And why does that make me feel so uneasy?

"I don't know. I guess you're easy to talk to." He shrugs. "I don't open up too often to people."

"You don't?" Because he is definitely opening up to me.

"I keep to myself mostly. Only have a few close friends."

"I understand." I'm pretty much the same. I knew lots of people in high school, but only a handful would I consider my real friends. Since I got kicked out of the house and couldn't maintain my old lifestyle, all of those friends have abandoned me. So I guess they weren't real friends after all.

I've dated a few guys, but only two did I actually do the deed with. And the first one doesn't even count, because he took my virginity and then proceeded to dump me a week later.

The asshole.

"But I'm the one who's talked the whole night. You've hardly said anything," Wade points out.

Uh oh.

"I don't mind listening," I say brightly, hoping to distract him. "Keep talking."

"I think it's your turn."

"Maybe I don't want it to be my turn."

He frowns. "Why not? You got secrets you want to hide?"

Wade

"I don't have any secrets," Sydney says, her voice in full on defense mode.

Huh. That makes me think she definitely has secrets she wants to hide. I can tell by the way her gaze cuts away from mine, the closed off expression on her face. But what could she be hiding? I really don't know much about her beyond her parents and their shitty marriage. Oh, and that she's from Texas and California and everywhere else. Talk about a vague answer. She's completely closed off while I just spilled my guts like she's my psychologist.

I don't normally do this—reveal so much. I can't even blame alcohol for loosening my lips. I'm stone cold sober tonight, preferring to keep my head on straight what with the game tomorrow. So what gives? Why did I tell Sydney all about my past, then go off rails about attraction, like I want to get with her?

Because maybe you do want to get with her? She's beautiful. She seems into you. You could probably have her naked and in your bed within the hour.

"I just don't have much to tell," Sydney continues, trying to play it off, I'm sure. "I'm not very interesting."

"Now I doubt that." When her gaze meets mine, I say, "I find you very interesting."

Yeah, I'm trying to dig for information, but I'm also speaking the truth. I do think she's interesting. Her mysterious ways only adds to my interest.

"The most exciting thing that's ever happened to me is what's going down right now." At my raised brows she continues. "The fake dating. Working for Drew and Fable. Ever since I started this job, my life has gotten a little crazy."

It hits me all of a sudden, everything that she's gone through. I think of all the stories that have appeared all over the Internet involving her and Drew. They've said some pretty terrible things about her. Called her all sorts of names. I can't imagine going through something like that.

"Are you holding up okay?" I ask softly.

She nods, dropping her gaze. "It hasn't been easy, but Drew and Fable have been so good to me. And so have you. We all know the truth, and I guess that's all that really matters."

The waiter chooses that moment to show up at our table to ask if we want dessert. I cut him off mid-sentence and ask for the check, which he sets on the edge of the table. I grab it, pulling my wallet out and placing my credit card within the small black blinder. The waiter smiles blandly and takes it from me and I nod distractedly, not caring about what else he has to say.

I want to hear what else *Sydney* has to say.

"What about your parents?" I ask once the waiter has left. "Have you heard from them?"

"My dad won't even acknowledge me right now. And my mother leaves me all sorts of voicemails. Sends me text messages, even writes me emails, but I still haven't responded, despite my brother reassuring me she's not mad, more worried."

"You should let her know you're okay," I suggest.

"Honestly? I don't know what to say to her. I'm afraid she won't let me explain and the next thing you know, we're arguing. That's how it usually goes between us." Her tone is bitter, as is her expression. I feel bad for her.

I also can't imagine having such unsupportive parents.

"Give them time," I suggest. "She'll come around eventually."

"Maybe. My brother has been great, but I knew he would be. We take care of each other."

"At least you have him, right?"

"Definitely." She lifts her head, her gaze meeting mine once more. "He's a good guy. Like you're a good guy."

"You think I'm a good guy?"

"You seem like one."

"I have my moments. Both good and bad."

"Don't we all?"

"True." I nod. "I'm always honest. That's one thing you can always count on. No bullshit here."

"Right," she says weakly. "No bullshit."

Huh.

The waiter reappears, returning my credit card and receipt. I add the tip and sign it before shoving my credit card back into my wallet.

"You ready to go?" I ask Sydney.

"Yeah." She smiles, looking nervous. "Sure."

We leave the restaurant, her hand clasped firmly in mine. The moment we exit the building, there are photographers there, a handful of them rushing forward, their camera flashes popping, making it hard to see. I throw my free hand up, blocking the light as I grip Sydney's hand tightly and push our way through the small crowd. They're all talking to her, asking her a list of questions like:

"It's the Naughty Nanny! Where's Drew?"

"Already moved onto a new guy?"

"Do you still work for the Callahans?

"Who's the guy, Syd? What's his name?"

"Trying to shed that naughty nanny image, Sydney?"

Every one of them is an asshole. I'm tempted to turn and sock them all in the face with my clutched fist.

"Don't say anything," Sydney whispers fiercely as we keep walking. "They're just trying to provoke me."

"I don't want to say anything," I tell her. "I want to hit them."

Her gaze meets mine and she laughs, keeping her steps hurried. She wants away from them as much as I do. "That would be even worse, though I appreciate you wanting to come to my defense."

"They're awful. I can't believe the stuff they say."

"And these guys are being mild."

It doesn't feel like they're being mild, but whatever. I gave the valet my ticket before we even left the restaurant and my truck magically appears, filling me with relief. I press a twenty-dollar bill in the valet's hand and hold open the passenger door for Sydney so she can climb into the truck. I shut the door just as the reporters descend upon me and they immediately launch into even more questions.

I whirl on them, putting on my most fierce face. "Y'all need to get the hell away from here and leave us alone."

"Who are you?" A guy with a camera slung around his neck steps forward, his expression defiant. "What's your name?"

Here's my chance to set the record straight. My chance to tell the new narrative we're trying to turn into the truth. "I'm Wade Knox—Sydney's boyfriend."

Oh, they all rush forward then, a few of them with their phones poised as if they're going to record me. The others have their big cameras in hand, ready to shoot about ten million photos.

I tell them we've been going out for about a month, that I'm newly drafted with the 49ers and that Fable is an old family friend. They eat up every word I say, asking question upon question until I finally give up and tell them I'm done. Without another word I climb into the truck, settle behind the steering wheel and start the engine.

"Did you really just talk to those reporters?" Sydney asks, sounding incredulous.

"I really just did."

"Why?"

I turn to look at her. "I told them I was your boyfriend. Fed them a tiny bit of information about myself and that was it." When she continues to just stare at me, I wonder if I somehow made a mistake. "That's what I was supposed to do, right? Bait them with new information so they'll talk about our relationship versus your supposed affair with Drew?"

She seems to mentally shake herself into agreeing. "Yes, of course. I'm sure that was a smart move."

So why does she act like what I just did was the worse move ever?

"You don't sound so confident."

Sydney sighs and I glance in the rearview mirror, noticing that the reporters are surrounding the back end of my truck. If they don't move out of the way, I'm going to end up hitting one of them. And wouldn't that suck?

"Now they know your name. They're going to dig into your background, search for any bit of dirt they can find," she says.

"They can't find any dirt on me," I say with confidence.

Though the longer I think about it, the more worried I become. I don't have a squeaky clean past, but I don't have a criminal background either. What if they root up a few vengeful girls who make me look like an asshole? Hell, what if they talk to Des, who'll say he was my and Owen's ex-roommate while we were in college and he also happens to be a fucking drug dealer?

Okay. There's the criminal element. I could look like I'm into some deep shit if they find Des. And then that'll *get* me into some deep shit, stuff I don't want to deal with.

"Trust me, even if they don't have any dirt on you, they can take something small and make it sound dirty," she warns.

"Don't forget. I've learned my lesson the hard way."

I look in the rearview mirror again, the reporters still there, lingering around like they want to capture a moment. My gaze drifts to Sydney, who's sitting in the passenger seat looking uptight as hell. She needs to loosen up. I blame the reporters. I think they make her nervous.

The girl needs to relax.

"Hey," I say softly, catching her attention. "Come here."

She frowns. "Come where?"

Crooking my finger at her, I indicate I want her to come toward me. She scoots a little closer, leaning over the center console that separates us and I take my advantage. I slip my hand around her nape and pull her face close to mine so our mouths are aligned.

Sydney flicks her surprised gaze up to mine, but before she can say anything, I silence her.

With my lips.

And holy hell, this girl tastes like absolute heaven, just like I knew she would. I cup her cheek with my hand, caressing her silky smooth skin. Her plush lips are sweet and warm, and undeniably soft. I kiss her once. Twice. The third time, she parts her lips slightly, letting me taste her better, inviting me, but I don't take my full opportunity. I can't push her too hard, not with witnesses watching.

What if my actions backfire and she freaks out on me and does something crazy? Like slap my face? Scream at me and call me a fucking asshole? We'd be totally screwed.

No way can I take that chance. I gotta be careful.

I finally break the kiss first, pulling away from her mouth

slightly and she snaps her lids open, staring at me in wonder. "What was that for?" she whispers.

"For them." I tilt my head, indicating the reporters outside. And maybe I kissed her a little for me, too. Just to test her out. See what it was like—kissing her.

It was pretty damn good.

Forget that.

It was fucking amazing.

chapter
Ten

Sydney

It's way too early on a Saturday morning. I forgot to close the blinds last night before I went to bed, so the bright morning sun is shining into my room like an unwanted intruder, illuminating the entire space with too much cheerful light. Groaning, I roll over and pull one of my pillows along with me, covering my head and blocking out the light. I just want to go back to sleep, though I doubt that's going to happen.

I barely slept last night. Instead I tossed and turned. All I could think about was Wade kissing me. What a casual gesture it had been, almost like an afterthought. How he called me to him, leaned over the console and pressed his lips to mine, never bothering to give me a warning that he was going to actually kiss me. Like it was no big deal. He just—did it, and threw me for a complete loop.

I'd been so startled at first, I didn't know how to react. I hadn't reacted, period. I just remained completely still, his perfectly warm lips gently coaxing mine to respond.

And then…gradually…I did respond. I automatically wanted more. So much more…

When he pulled away seconds later, I had to fight the disappointment that threatened to overwhelm me. It was over. He acted like what just happened was no big deal. That the kiss we just shared had merely been a part of our agreement while I sat there blinking up at him like a dork, thoroughly confused. What we're doing is supposed to be fake.

So why did that kiss feel so damn real?

That's why I couldn't sleep last night. After all that talk about love and what a crock of shit it is, how relationships are nothing but trouble, he goes and kisses me like he means it and makes me want things I can't have.

I have no one to talk to about any of this with either. No way can I turn to Fable. She'll think I'm pitiful for hoping what Wade and I are doing might turn into something…I don't know…

Real?

Yeah. Can't go to her. Can't go to Gabe either. He wouldn't understand. First of all, he's a guy. Second of all, he's my brother. Yikes. Third of all, he doesn't know how to give advice, or even listen for very long. Yes, his girlfriend Lucy has softened him, but he's still my impatient, all-knowing brother.

So instead I let the thoughts eat me up inside. Until I can't stand it anymore and I leap out of bed, taking a shower and getting ready for my day so I can spend time with little Jacob and Autumn. Fable told me I could sleep in and that I only had to work a half-day taking care of the kids. Eventually we're all going to the game together, though Fable will be watching it from the skybox with the children. I'll be down in the stands and close to the field — as close as I can get, according to Drew and Wade. They want me to put on a big show, rooting for my new boyfriend and making a scene.

It's kind of lame, how excited I am to put on this big show just for my supposed man. The man who isn't mine at all — but I'm pretending he is.

Ugh.

If I think about this for too long, I'll realize just how lame and extremely pitiful it really is. What we're doing is ridiculous. Worse? I can't stop thinking about him. Ever since that kiss — which really wasn't that big of a deal in the grand scheme of kissing — Wade Knox has consumed my thoughts.

Completely.

There's a knock on my bedroom door just as I'm coming out of the en suite bathroom. I've already taken my shower and I'm dressed, though I haven't dried my hair or put on makeup yet. I go to answer the door, but it opens before I can get there.

Wade barges in, looking sheepish as he closes the door behind him. "Hey. Good morning." He leans against the door, his gaze wandering the length of me and making me warm.

"You're lucky I wasn't naked," I tell him, resting my hands on my hips, pretending to be annoyed. I'm trying to be pissed that he just barged in here before making sure it was okay, but really I'm flat out thrilled to see him in my room. It's like I conjured him up in my thoughts and he magically appeared. And I'm not protesting.

Wade seems to eat up all the space with his massive

presence, until he becomes all I can see.

"I don't know about that," he drawls, making me blush. Ugh, this man. I can't let myself fall for him.

I can't.

"Why are you here?"

"I had to show you what's going on. Figured you'd want to know." He takes a tentative step, and when I don't run for it, he shifts closer, until he's standing right beside me with his phone in his hands and he's scrolling, looking for something. "Here, check this out."

Wade hands me his phone. He's pulled up the TMZ webpage, and there's a photo of the two of us together from last night, leaving the restaurant. The small article that accompanies the photo states that the Naughty Nanny has already found a new boyfriend—and that would be Wade Knox, an old family friend of Drew and Fable Callahan's, and a recently drafted player for the Niners.

That naughty nanny thing is such crap. It's humiliating, how they won't let that go.

"See? It worked!" he says excitedly, taking his phone back from me. "I knew my talking to them would help. Seeing us together helped too, but letting them know who I am was the right thing to do."

"But they still called me the freaking 'Naughty Nanny'," I point out, using air quotes just like Fable did a few days ago. "They also mentioned I was caught having an affair with Drew, which is a total lie. They're never going to let that go."

I try not to sound all doom and gloom but hello. I'm feeling pretty doom and gloom right about now. Despite the fact I have a gorgeous, sexy man in my bedroom. I should be thrilled.

But we're in a fake relationship. This is all…bogus.

So why doesn't it feel bogus? It should. I don't want to get my hopes up.

Too late. They're already up.

"We need to amp it up, and then trust me, they will definitely let all that bullshit go," he says, his dark eyes sparkling. Why is he so cheerful this early in the morning? I sort of hate him right now. That's because I desperately need coffee. "We need to put on a big display at the game tonight."

"How?" I go and sit on the edge of my still unmade bed, and oh my God…

Wade sits down right next to me, making the mattress squeak from his weight. He's sitting so close and he's so hot—figuratively and literally. I'm still a little steamed up from the shower I took earlier, so he's not helping matters. At all. Plus, this feels so intimate, him in my room, sitting on my unmade bed, and it's not even nine o'clock in the morning. If I let my imagination run wild, I could almost envision us being like this after he stayed the night. In my bed.

Though I'd rather still be *in* my bed. With Wade. Naked.

Oh. God. My thoughts have seriously gone off the rails.

"We need to act like we're totally into each other," he says, his face, his voice deadly serious.

"Okaaaay."

"Like, *way* into each other," he stresses, his gaze never straying from mine.

"Uh huh." That won't be a hardship, especially after last night's kiss.

"It needs to be undeniable, how much we want each other."

"And how do you propose we do that?" I ask, getting a little irritated. I seriously don't know what he expects me to do when he's out on that field playing the game tonight and I'm sitting up in the stands.

"Well, maybe we should run through a few things and practice first." He scoots even closer, his thigh nudging against mine. It's solid with muscle, and wide, and I'm tempted to reach out and touch it. Touch him. Just rest my hand on his thigh, slip my fingers beneath the hem of his dark blue athletic shorts and see how muscular he really is....

I clear my throat, hoping that'll also clear my head. "What do you think we should practice?"

"I've been thinking about you—uh, *this* all last night. And how we can make this appear even more real between us."

Oh wow. He's been thinking about me? Maybe I kept him up all night too, like he did to me. Maybe he's feeling the same exact way about me that I feel about him, which is...

Crap. I don't know how I feel about him. I just know that I like him, and that I'm attracted to him.

And he said he was a big believer in attraction...

"Tell me how we can make this pretend thing between us seem more real," I say my voice low and hopefully sexy.

"We can push it to the next level." He tucks a wet strand of hair behind my ear, making me shiver. "We can do little things, like me touching your hair. Those kinds of gestures make us seem like a bona fide couple."

I give in to my earlier urge and rest my hand on top of his thigh, though I don't dive beneath his shorts like I wanted to.

That would be too much. Right? "Do you mean like this?"

"Uh." His gaze drops to my hand on his thigh. "Yeah. Like that," he says to my hand.

I give him a firm squeeze. He's solid as a rock, I swear. I run my hand down until I'm touching his bare knee, his soft leg hair tickling my palm, and I'm suddenly tempted to do more exploring. More searching. My hands are literally itching to stroke all over his body. We have the time. I don't have to be downstairs until ten, or maybe even later. We can give in to all of this attraction bubbling between us and just…let it take over.

Forget the emotional component of all of this. Emotions have nothing to do with what I'm feeling toward him.

"Sydney…" he starts, but this time I'm the one with the advantage. I go up on my knees so I'm more level with his mouth and kiss him. I grab hold of his shoulders and hang on for dear life as I press my mouth on his once. Twice. Soft, lingering kisses that last longer and longer, until our lips are parted and his tongue sneaks out to trace my upper lip.

It's like we've given ourselves permission to just go for it, so we do. The kiss is instantly hot. Deep. Wet. Tangling tongues and hot breaths. I somehow end up on his lap, straddling him, clinging to his shoulders, rubbing against him like I've lost all inhibitions. I'm wearing tiny denim shorts and a tank top and his hands are on my butt, gripping me, pulling me in close so I can feel him.

And yeah. He's big. Erect. I can't believe it.

I want more of it. More of him.

He breaks the kiss first and starts in on my neck, his lips hot and damp as they slide over my sensitive skin. "Christ, you smell good," he whispers.

There's a knock on the door and I look up to watch as it swings open and there's Fable, standing in the doorway with wide eyes and her mouth hanging open. I tear my lips away from Wade's, my hands in his hair, his hands on my butt, both of us wrapped around each other so tight you couldn't fit a piece of paper in between us.

Oops.

"Ohmigosh! Sorry, sorry, sorry!" Fable scrambles out of my room and slams the door shut so hard, everything rattles.

Great.

Wade

"I bet we looked pretty convincing just now," I mutter as I lift Sydney off my lap and set her on the edge of the bed.

She runs her hands over her damp hair, her head averted so…what? She doesn't have to look at me? Hell. "I'm probably going to lose my job."

"Why? Because we're pretending to be a couple and we got a little too into it for a few minutes? No way. I won't let it happen." I rise to my feet, ready to go talk to Fable and explain what happened. I do a quick dick check, and yep, my erection disappeared the moment we heard Fable's panicked voice.

Talk about a mood changer. More like talk about a mood accelerator. The moment I sat next to Sydney on her bed, I had visions of laying her out on the mattress and getting her naked. I touched her hair, she touched my thigh, and then it was on.

But the way she's acting now, not looking at me, all fluttery nervousness, I'm wondering if I read her wrong after all.

"Hey." I touch her shoulder and she jumps, turning to finally look at me. The worry and guilt written all over her expressive face tugs at my heart. "Are you all right?"

She nods and rises to her feet so she's standing in front of me, but she only reaches me about mid-chest. She's so tiny. When I cupped her perfect ass in my hands just moments ago I realized just how small she is.

"I'm fine," she says, her voice a little shaky. "I just—I don't want Fable mad at me. Us."

"She won't be," I say firmly. "They're the ones who asked us to do this. How could we not get close after pretending to be a couple?"

"Yeah, but we've accelerated from zero to one hundred in about two-point-five seconds. What just happened felt crazy fast."

"Too fast?" When she frowns I continue. "You don't feel like I pushed you too hard, do you?"

"No, never." Sydney shakes her head. "I'm the one who threw myself at you."

"Not quite." I run a hand through my hair and take a deep breath, trying to calm my racing heart. I'm agitated, my blood fiery hot as it pumps through my veins. What just happened— that kiss—blew my freaking mind.

This girl has come out of nowhere and rocked my world with a few choice words, a handful of touches and a kiss that's making me reevaluate every other kiss I've ever experienced.

Which is fucking crazy, right? I just met this girl. I know nothing about her. Plus, she's too young, and I'm too young, and I don't want anything serious. This isn't serious. Hell, it's fake.

Fake.

Fake.

Fake.

Doesn't feel like it, though. The energy radiating between us at this very moment is palpable. I need to get out of here. Need to go to Fable and make this right.

"I'm gonna talk to Fable and straighten everything out, all right?" I grab hold of Sydney's arm, and it's like my fingers catch on fire just from touching her. The girl affects me like no other. "You sure you okay?"

She nods, a hunk of damp hair falling in front of her face, and I'm tempted to tuck it behind her ear again. But I resist. Barely. "I'm fine."

Giving in to my urges, I kiss her one more time. Just a brief peck on the lips, but damn if I didn't feel that quick touch stir something deep inside my soul.

Ridiculous.

I flee her room before I do something stupid like kiss her again, and she doesn't stop me. Good. I need some time alone just to reevaluate what happened. Even if it is only a few minutes walking down the stairs in search of Fable, at least I'm alone with my thoughts—my overloaded brain that's filled with all sorts of crazy images. Images like me and Sydney together—for real.

As if I have time to try out this dating thing. My life is about to change completely, as long as everything unfolds as planned. I'll be traveling constantly for away games. I'll never be home because I'll be working so hard. Practicing all the time. It's not fair to ask a woman to stand by my side and deal with my hectic life. I need to remain single.

I think of Owen, who is definitely not single. I think of Drew, who's been with Fable since he was twenty-one and has zero regrets. Hell, Owen's been with Chelsea since he was nineteen. Were they always believers in love? Or did the women they met change their perspectives?

Fable's in the kitchen cutting apple slices and she barely looks in my direction when I enter the room. "Want a snack?" she asks.

"No," I say firmly. "Want to talk?"

She lifts her head, her gaze meeting mine. "Do you?"

"I do." I take a seat on one of the barstools at the kitchen counter. "Should I apologize for what just happened?"

"Of course you don't have to apologize," she says. "I was just—taken aback at first. I had no idea you two were, uh, feeling that way. I thought what was happening with you guys was all phony, just as we planned."

"It *is* fake," I say, ignoring the skeptical look on Fable's face. "I'm serious. We just got—carried away."

"Uh huh. What were you doing in her room anyway, Wade?" A brow goes up and she sets the knife on the cutting board so she can cross her arms. I wouldn't doubt for an instant she's tapping her foot, too.

Ah damn, she sounds and looks like the Fable of old, who would constantly bust our balls and make Owen and I feel guilty for all the crazy shit we used to do. We deserved to feel that way because we were always up to no good, but we hated it so much when she ripped us a new one.

That's because she was so damn good at it. Just like that, I'm back to being fourteen years old and I just got caught making out a little too heavily with Jessica Fairchild in Owen's bedroom. On Owen's bed, with my hand on Jessica's right tit and Jessica trying to shove me off her when she spotted Fable fuming in the doorway. Fable busted me hard, ratted me out to my mom and everything. I was so pissed at her for weeks. Every one of those days I was grounded, I cursed her existence over and over again.

Now I'm so glad she was there, watching out for me. I was wild, but I could've been worse. Much worse. Fable helped keep me and Owen grounded.

"I came over to show Sydney what the media was saying about the two of us," I say in my defense.

Fable's eyes light up and her arms drop to her sides. "Oh, what are they saying? Is it positive?"

Relief floods me at the change of subject. I'm thankful I could cheer her up. An angry Fable is an unpleasant Fable let me tell you.

Whipping out my phone, I show Fable the TMZ article. "They talked about us."

She reads the article, nibbling on her lower lip. "They won't let go of the Naughty Nanny thing, though."

Yeah, she sounds just like Sydney with that comment. "We'll get them to forget about it."

"You really think you two can do that in just than a week's time?" She sounds skeptical, and that doesn't help my confidence.

"You're the one who said it would only take a week," I point out.

"I know. And a lot of things can happen in a week, trust me. I mean, look at you two."

"What about us two?" I frown.

"I already caught you kissing her in her bedroom, just like when you were a teenager." She grins.

I feel my cheeks heat with embarrassment. I'm a grown ass man. I shouldn't let that sort of thing bother me. "We sort of lost our minds."

"Does she make you lose your mind?"

This conversation needs to come to a halt, so I decide to change the direction. "How are you feeling?"

"Nice subject changer." Fable shakes her head. "I'm feeling all right. The baby is sapping all the energy right out of me."

"I can't believe you're pregnant again."

"I can't believe it either, but this is a good thing. Drew and I want a big family. So this baby is an unexpected blessing. I just need to take it easy." She runs a quick hand over her still-flat belly. "The timing isn't the best, but everything will work out in the end."

I say nothing. I wonder if that's the attitude I should take about this thing with Sydney. That everything will work out in the end, no matter what happens. It's better than worrying about shit all the time. We should just let nature take its course.

Yeah. That sounds good. Nature taking its course. Either it works or it doesn't.

I'm secretly hoping it works.

chapter
Eleven

Sydney

According to Fable, the preseason games usually aren't very crowded, but this particular one brought out a lot of Niner fans tonight, and I'm fairly certain it's because Drew's playing. He normally doesn't play much during the preseason schedule because they let the second and third string players have the opportunity to show everyone what they can do. But tonight is an exception. It's the last game of the preseason, and Drew needs to show off his skills to get the fans hyped for the regular season. And he's played amazingly well — no surprise.

Wade has done well too. He's spent the majority of the game actually playing it. They only pulled him off the field once, right before halftime. But the moment the third quarter started, he was back out on that field, playing like his life depended on it. He even caught one of Drew's passes and ran it into the end zone, scoring a touchdown, making me hop up and down and scream my head off.

The photographers clicked away, documenting my overhyped reaction, but I ignored them as best as I could.

I've tried my best to be the perfect girlfriend tonight. If the various reporters are watching me, and I'm sure some of them are, I look like the good little woman out in support of her man. Oh, I'm sure a few of them will twist the story around and say I'm really cheering for Drew, but whatever. I'm starting to realize we can't win with them.

That article Wade shared with me cemented my feelings. How am I ever going to shed the Naughty Nanny nickname when they won't let it go? It's everywhere still, and I bet no matter how much time passes, they'll still call me that. I might *never* be able to shake it.

And that would be awful.

When the game's finished, I go down onto the field thanks to the all-access pass Fable obtained for me before we left the house for the game. She texted me when there was two minutes left in the fourth quarter—the Niners eventually won the game—to let me know she'd meet me on the field. She and Drew had privately arranged a quick photo session with the entire family involved, just to please the media and hopefully get them to shut up about the nanny gossip. I hope it works, considering I potentially benefit from this photo opp too.

The moment I walk onto the field, I spot the Callahans posing for the cameras and I go in the opposite direction, not wanting to interfere, and not wanting to look like I'm lurking around them either. I go and search for Wade instead, and I find him standing on the sidelines, chatting with his teammates and what looks like a couple of reporters. The reporters try to ask them questions, but they're all laughing and giving each other a hard time.

Giving me the chance to wait patiently and admire him.

Which isn't a hardship. He looks amazing in his uniform, those tight gold (fine, I know gold isn't a great color, but Wade makes it work) pants clinging to his thick thighs, his brown hair a sweaty mess, the black lines beneath his eyes smudged, his helmet dangling from his fingers. He's broad and tall and imposing and I remember what it was like this morning, sitting in his lap on my bed, my mouth fused with his and wrapped all around him. He's so incredibly masculine and delicious, and I can't believe I have to pretend he's all mine.

I sort of want him to *be* all mine. No questions asked.

Like that's ever really going to happen.

When he spots me, it's like the air shifts and all the hairs on my body stand on end. I can feel his gaze lingering on my body, and I turn my head to find him watching me, a pleased smile on his handsome face when his dark gaze meets mine. He says goodbye to the guys and then makes his way toward me, his easy, confident stride making me die a little inside.

I could watch him approach me like that all damn day.

Wade stops directly in front of me that smile still stretching his lips wide. "Hey."

"Hi." That's all I can come up with. My brain is just—blank.

"So. What did you think?" When I frown, he continues. "Of the game."

"Oh!" *Duh.* He must think I'm an idiot. "You played

wonderfully. And when you caught the ball and ran in that touchdown in the third quarter..."

He grins, pleased with himself. "I know, right? It was pretty fucking awesome."

"Wade!" He always seems to watch himself around me. He's very careful. Respectful. So I'm not used to him dropping f-bombs. Not that I care. My brother and his friends curse all the time, so it never really bothers me. Still. "You shouldn't curse in public."

"Ha. Get used to it," he mutters before he hauls me in close and gives me a blistering kiss.

I lose myself in that kiss. There's plenty of tongue and heat, and one strong arm is wrapped tight around my waist, his large hand palming my butt. He's got on all the pads and equipment still so I can't really feel him, but that's okay.

He still feels pretty damn amazing.

"Think they got enough photos of us kissing just now?" he whispers against my lips a few minutes later. I crack open my eyes to find him watching me and I stare up at him blankly. "Well? Do you?"

Reality crashes down upon me, reminding me that yes that amazing kiss was completely bogus and I need to get my head out of the clouds.

Withdrawing from his embrace, I nod, needing the distance. I'm all shaky. My body feels like it's been electrified just by his lips — and his hand on my butt — and I don't know if I can walk straight. Let alone think straight.

"Oh yeah. I'm sure they did."

He smiles. "Good. Just keeping with the plan."

"Right." I nod. Take a shaky breath, then letting it out in an equally shaky exhale. He's turned me into a total mess and he has no clue his effect on me.

In fact, he's downright oblivious. He's already thinking ahead, talking about our plans tonight, which aren't real. They're just some put on thing to give the media-slash-stalkers something to talk about. "Give me some time to shower and change and then I'll be out. Is that okay?"

As if I have any right to demand something else. I'm not really his girlfriend, after all. "That's fine."

"Fable's still around to hang out with, right?" When I nod, Wade does too. "Cool. I don't like thinking of you out here all alone. See you in a bit." He drops a kiss on the tip of my nose and then walks away, but I don't watch him go.

Why torture myself? I'm twisted up enough.

I'm about to make my escape and go in search of Fable when a man wearing a red T-shirt with a 49ers emblem emblazed on the front and a pair of pressed khaki shorts stops directly in front of me, a friendly smile on his face.

"Hi." He sends me a knowing look. "Well, look at you."

"Um, hi," I say in return, tilting my head to the side, trying to figure out if I know him. Considering the social circles my parents moved in, I've met a lot of people over the years. Maybe I know this guy?

Or maybe not. He's sort of—odd. The way he's staring at me, like he's trying to figure me out. It's unsettling.

"You're Sydney Walker, right?"

"Yes?" I'm dying to say *who's asking,* but I remain quiet. I don't want to be rude. And there's no need in making this any more uncomfortable than it already is. "Can I help you with anything?"

What's this guy's deal anyway?

"Just making sure you're who I thought you were, and you are. Nice kiss, by the way. Great distraction you've got going on, this so-called newfound relationship you're having with the new kid. Though none of it is for real. We all know the truth about you and Callahan." He smirks and then strides away, never once looking back. I'm left watching him leave, wondering who the hell he was, and who he might work for.

That asshole was a reporter.

We are so screwed.

Wade

"So wait a minute. Some random dude came up to you on the field after I left you and said he doesn't believe our relationship is real?" I clench my teeth together, my jaw going tight. "Who was he?"

We're at an Italian restaurant not too far from the stadium, having a late dinner. There are a ton of Niners fans in here, but none of them recognize me so they all leave us alone.

"I don't know. He didn't say his name and he was wearing a Niners T-shirt. He could be anybody." She sighs, the sound so desolate, so sad, I'm tempted to grab her, pull her into my arms and give her a comforting hug.

"What an asshole." I shake my head, getting more heated up the longer I think about it. "I can't believe he said that to you."

"He seemed real pleased when he said it too. Like he knew his words would shock me." She hesitates before she whispers, "They hurt me too."

Anger makes my blood run hot. "If I ever find him, I'm gonna kill that bastard."

"Please. It's okay. Calm down." Sydney reaches across the table and touches my forearm, her cool fingers pressing into my skin. Despite my growing rage, I can admit her touch soothes me. "He was probably nobody important. I'm sure we have nothing to worry about."

Her words aren't registering. I'm too pissed. "I can't believe you chose to wait and tell me this until we got to the restaurant. Why didn't you tell me about that guy when we were still at the stadium? Maybe we could've found him," I say incredulously. "At the very least, you should've said something in the car on the way over here."

"I didn't want to make a big deal about this. He could've been anyone just trying to get a dig in," she says.

"Well, it worked. Now I want to dig into his face and pulverize it." I shake my head and grab the glass of beer in front of me, taking a sip. I thought I'd indulge for once tonight, especially since I learned I am officially on the 49ers roster for the season. Talk about having something to celebrate. I was feeling on top of the world until Sydney told me what happened to her with that jerk guy saying what he did.

"I didn't want to put you in a bad mood. I know how excited you are tonight and I didn't want to ruin it." She rubs my arm, her fingers squeezing me tight. "I'm so proud of you."

Is that really Sydney talking? Or is she putting on a show

for everyone else? No one is sitting nearby. We're in a pretty intimate booth in the far corner of the restaurant, so no one can hear us.

I want to believe she's proud of me. I need to hear those words tonight. I've worked too damn long and hard not to feel good about my newest accomplishment.

"Thanks," I mutter, taking another sip of my beer. While we still have intensive practice five days a week for hours at a time, we don't have an official game for another two weeks. If I want to cut loose for the remainder of the weekend, I don't see how it can hurt.

Sydney sighs and takes her hand away from my arm. I immediately miss her touch. "Listen, don't even think about that guy tonight. Who cares about all that stuff? We're doing what we can to help out Drew and Fable, and hopefully reporters will take the bait and eventually leave us alone. If not, then— then I don't know what we can do to change their minds."

"If we can't change their minds, we'll have to ride out the storm, I guess," I offer, sending her a look.

She frowns, but she's still so damn pretty, even when she's upset. "I hate that our lives are at the mercy of other people. It's like rude reporters and asshole photographers rule the world."

"Only if you let them control you," I say, chuckling under my breath. I like how she called them asshole photographers. Her description is pretty damn accurate.

"Well, I guess I'm letting them control me then. Aren't you?" She narrows her eyes, her expression challenging.

"Nah." I wave a hand, trying to act more casual than I feel. "I'm going to do what I want regardless of what any of them say."

"It's not like you can do *whatever* you want right now, you know what I mean? We're putting on this phony show for the entire world to watch. Don't you think that's kind of — weird?"

Looks like someone is analyzing her current situation a little too closely.

"It's only as weird as you make it," I reassure her. "Or you can just run with this plan and have fun while it lasts."

"Is that what you're doing? Having fun?" she asks, her voice low.

So I lower mine too. "Isn't that what we were doing in your bedroom earlier? Having a little fun?" I tap the back of her hand with my index finger, but she snatches it away. Aw, she's blushing. Damn, she's cute when she does that.

"Stop."

"Stop what?" I rest a hand on my chest, always Mr. Innocent. It's a lot more interesting to talk about what's going on between us than worry over what some jackass reporter is up to. "What exactly am I doing?"

"Bringing up what happened this morning."

"What happened this morning was not only fun, but also pretty damn hot, you have to admit." It's all I've been able to think about for the remainder of the day. Even during the game, I thought about Sydney. Her taste, the little whimper that sounded low in her throat when I grabbed her ass, how responsive she was. I swear I was a better player out on that field tonight while thinking about her.

Almost like she spurred me on.

"It was — good." That's all she says. Well, and her pink

cheeks say a million words too, none of them she's actually speaking out loud.

"Did you enjoy it?"

Sydney blinks those pretty blue eyes up at me, and I feel like I can see a myriad of emotions sparkling within them. Not a one of them I can decipher either, and that makes me uneasy. "It wasn't real, right?"

Her question stumps me. No, it wasn't real. Yet...it was. It *felt* real. Her tongue was in my mouth. My tongue was in her mouth. We were touching each other. Hell, she was practically grinding on me and gave me an immediate hard on. If that's not real, I don't know what is. "What exactly do you mean?"

"What happened between us this morning, I think we just got—caught up in a moment." She nods, like her explanation makes all the sense in the world. More like she just convinced herself it makes sense. "Yeah, that's all it was. A total moment we got caught up in."

She's repeating herself. Making me wonder if she's still caught up in a so-called moment.

"What about last night in my truck?" I give in and touch her again. Just drift my fingers along her bare forearm, my fleeting touch making goose flesh dot her skin. Thank Christ the tables are small so I can reach her easily. "What was that?"

"For the cameras."

Ouch. Sydney's brutal right now. "And what about earlier? Right after the game?"

"For the cameras again. This is *all* for the cameras. Remember our agreement, Wade? We're putting on one big performance to save my ass from being called the 'Naughty Nanny' ever again.

And to keep Drew and Fable's image squeaky clean." She pulls away from my touch as she slides out of the booth until she's standing by the end of the table. "I'm going to the restroom."

Without another word she leaves and I watch her go, fighting the disappointment that wants to wash over me. She's mad. At me? I sure as hell hope not, but maybe she is. I don't know what's going on, but she seems on edge. I'm sure the encounter with that asshole on the field earlier doesn't help matters. I think all this pretending is starting to get to her head.

I know it's gotten to both of mine.

chapter Twelve

Wade

Sydney's quiet the rest of the time we're at the restaurant. It's like she's thrown up an impenetrable wall that I can't push my way over, no matter what. She's responsive when she needs to be, answering my questions and keeping up with our polite yet stilted conversation, but otherwise, she's silent.

Eerily so.

It fucking sucks. There are no other words for it. Granted, I get that she's upset after what happened with the guy on the field, but I don't think that's the only thing bothering her. Something else is going on. Something I think that has to do with…

Me.

It's probably all this fake crap we're putting ourselves through. Maybe it really is messing with her head. Sydney and

I are compatible in the chemistry department, and maybe that's a problem for her. It might feel far too real.

I know I've experienced that once or twice. I've enjoyed it too, despite my knowing how it's all going to end.

And it *will* end. I can guarantee that.

After I pay the bill, we leave the restaurant and head back to Drew and Fable's house so I can drop Sydney off. I crank up the music on the truck radio—anything's better than the dead silence between us—and tap my fingers against the steering wheel, keeping the beat.

"You're good at that." When I look at her weirdly, she explains further. "Keeping rhythm. You're doing it perfectly."

I shrug, my gaze focused on the road ahead. If I look at her for too long, I might get distracted. And I don't need that right now, especially since I'm driving. Thank Christ I didn't drink much beyond that one beer at dinner. My head is clear. I need to keep it that way. "Once upon a time, I wanted to be a drummer in a band."

"Why didn't you become one?"

"Who said I didn't try?" I slide her a quick glance.

"So you, what? Played drums in the school band?"

"In middle school," I say with a one-shoulder shrug.

Sydney bursts out laughing. "That doesn't count. What, you played in the band for two years? Three?"

"Four, if you count the fifth and sixth grade," I say indignantly, which only makes her laugh harder. "What's so funny?"

It takes her a few minutes to regain her composure, which in turn pisses me off even more. I can't even begin to explain why her reaction is upsetting me so much. "I can't imagine big, badass Wade Knox playing drums for the band in middle school."

"Well, it's true. I did play in the school band for four years," I stress. "Though I don't know if I'd call me big and bad back then. I was pretty small."

"Oops, sorry. So you were small, tiny Wade Knox playing the drums for the middle school band," Sydney says, barely able to contain her laughter.

"I don't see what the big deal is," I mutter, shaking my head.

"It's just…" She waits a moment for her laughter to die before she starts talking again. "I've been in middle school band. I know how that works. I'm going to guess you were a terrible player."

"I was great," I say, in full on defensive mode. "What instrument did you play?"

"Clarinet."

Worst instrument ever. "And I'm sure you sucked."

"Miserably. I didn't even last beyond sixth grade. Couldn't take it anymore and I begged my mom to let me quit. So she did." I can feel Sydney's gaze on me, but I don't turn to look her way. "Why did you quit the band?"

"Football. I couldn't do both, so I had to choose. I chose football." I scowl at the stretch of road before us. "Didn't regret that choice either."

"I'm sure." She shakes her head, giggling like she's a little girl in the middle of a laughing fit. "I don't know why I found that so funny."

"What, the fact that I was in the school band? I don't either, considering you were in band too, playing the stupid clarinet."

"Hey, don't insult my instrument choice. Lots of people play the clarinet," she says defensively.

"Badly."

"Aw, you're mad, aren't you? Don't be mad." She rests her hand on my knee for a too brief second before removing it. "I was just teasing you about your secret life as a band geek."

"Uh huh. And what deep dark secret do you have lingering in your murky past?" I ask, desperate to change the subject. Plus it would be nice to gather some ammo to use against her in the future.

"Nothing." She sits up straight, not even looking in my direction. "I'm squeaky clean. My clarinet years are the only secret I have."

I stay quiet for a while, enjoying watching her squirm. Because yes, she really is squirming over there in the passenger seat. I've barely said anything and I can tell she's uncomfortable. "Sure, that's your only secret," I finally drawl.

"For real." I glance over to find Sydney glaring at me, her pretty blue eyes narrowed and her expression fiery. "You're being really rude right now."

"Hey. I was only teasing." Damn, she's sensitive tonight. We're both a little touchy, I guess. This morning's kiss was probably a huge mistake. Now we're both wound up, snapping at each other, and that sucks. We still have a solid five days left of this plan.

How are we going to survive it?

"Fine," she murmurs after a few minutes of tense silence. "I do have a secret."

Shock courses through me. "You do?" I was just giving her shit. I didn't believe she was really hiding something.

"Yeah." Her voice is soft. "It's nothing major, I guess. Well, I don't like talking about it much, especially since it just happened."

"If you don't want to tell me, I understand. You don't have to," I say, the words rushing out of me. "It's none of my business. I was just teasing you."

"No, I want to tell you."

"You don't have to, though."

"But I want to."

No way do I want her to feel like I'm forcing her to tell me anything. We are on a need-to-know basis right now, and I can tell this is something I don't need to know. Just because we're playing at having a relationship doesn't mean we have to play true confessions. She's allowed her secrets.

Just like I'm allowed mine.

"Only if you want to tell me," I say. "Don't feel obligated."

"I don't. It's really not that big of a deal. There's no scandalous tale, no secret baby or anything like that," she says casually.

Meanwhile, my heart just did a double flip. "Secret baby?"

"Right. No babies. So don't be scared."

Yeah. The last thing I want to hear about is a secret baby. "What is it then?"

Sydney takes a deep breath and slowly lets it all out, sounding like a deflating tire. "My family is rich."

I let that sink in for a moment. She says nothing else, just leaves that one statement hanging in the air and I try to wrap my head around it.

"How rich are we talking?"

"Millionaire status." She pauses. "Millions and millions."

"Tens of millions?" Because holy shit.

"Hundreds of millions." Another hesitation. "They just kicked me out of the house."

Hundreds of millions? Damn. She's not just rich. She's *fucking* rich.

"Why'd they kick you out?" I'm angry all over again, but this time on her behalf. How could her parents kick her out of their home? They must be mean, heartless creatures who don't give a shit about their child. Who does that? Such bullshit.

"I lied to them."

I glance over to see she's staring at her lap, her gaze seemingly focused on her hand as she picks at the hole in the knee of her jeans.

"What about?"

"I said I was in college when I wasn't. I never applied to any universities because, at the time, I didn't care. I didn't want to go. I believed I didn't have to go, that my family's money would take care of me for life. Isn't that stupid?" She lifts her head, her gaze meeting mine, and I want to immediately tell her that no, it wasn't stupid.

If she'd gone on to college, we would've never met. If she'd gone on to college, she would be somewhere else. And I would've been here. Alone.

Without her.

But I say none of that, because I sound crazy.

Even in my own thoughts.

Sydney

Wade's not saying much, and his silence makes me want to snatch back the words I just said and shove them into a deep, dark hole. The words that make me sound dumb and irresponsible and so incredibly foolish. That's me in a nutshell.

And I hate myself for it.

"We all do dumb shit when we're seventeen, eighteen years old," he finally says, shooting me a sympathetic glance. "Don't beat yourself up over it."

"Kind of hard not to when my stupidity ruined everything," I say sarcastically. "I was dumb throughout high school. Not really dumb, I guess — more like spoiled. I thought I could get away with everything."

Oh, and I did. I got away with pretty much everything but murder. Smoking a joint in the girls' bathroom with my friends in between classes? Did that. TP'ing the principal's house the weekend before my junior year was finished for the summer? Yep, did that too. I cheated on tests, I stole this one girl's earrings because I thought they were beautiful and I wanted them. Then I promptly lost them not a week later. Once I got drunk with the basketball team in their locker room after a particularly brutal game and the coach found me stumbling around, close to passing out with all the guys watching me, leering at me. They probably had plans for me.

The coach saved me that night, and never breathed a word about that incident to anyone.

Yep, that all happened to me. You could've looked up risky

behavior in teens on the Internet, and my photo would've popped up. I did stupid stuff. Went to parties I shouldn't have gone to, messed around with boys who had bad reputations. Hung out with girls who had bad reputations too. I loved it. I strived hard for a bad reputation. I desperately wanted one.

The start of my senior year, my parents started nagging me about applying for college, and I didn't. My grades weren't the best. I didn't want to take the SATs—too boring. So I partied and I had fun and I got barely passing grades and when I graduated high school, all my friends had a plan. A purpose.

I had nothing.

"I guess that's what happens when you're handed everything you could ever want and you never have to earn it." I expected him to sound bitter, but he doesn't. I know he doesn't come from money, that he struggled and had to work hard for everything good that he has. My life was the complete opposite of his. He is what he is today because he worked for it.

I'm here, doing what I'm doing because I was forced to. This is not the life I expected, or wanted. If you asked me a year ago what I would be doing after high school, I would've answered, *"Partying with my friends, hooking up with cute boys and having the time of my life."*

None of that came true. My parents kicked me out. My friends ditched me. The boy I had been semi-seeing before I got the boot didn't bother responding to me when I sent multiple texts. I needed someone to lean on and he wouldn't even give me a second of his time. He was done. I was checked off his list.

I got checked off everyone's list.

"I'm the classic spoiled rotten rich girl who got everything taken away from me. I don't deserve any sympathy," I talk over him, cutting off whatever he'd been about to say. Maybe he was going to defend me, I don't know, but I didn't want to hear it. I've said and thought and used every excuse there is.

I'm done with excuses. I'm actually living my life now, and making my own choices. And it feels pretty good.

"You seem to be doing pretty good for yourself right now," Wade says, his deep voice quiet and soft.

"I got lucky. My brother helped me get this job. Now I just need to remain on the straight and narrow and keep it."

It's not hard to stay on the straight and narrow when you have no one to party with. And that's me, the ex-party girl who's now a complete loner. Yes, Fable treats me like a friend, but ultimately I'm her employee. And yes, I'm spending a lot of time with Wade, but every moment we're together isn't real.

It's fake.

"I don't think you give yourself enough credit," Wade says, making me want to laugh.

"I think you're giving me too much credit. You don't even know me."

"I can read people pretty well. You're not a bad person, Sydney."

"You're only saying that because you like kissing me." I can't believe I just said that.

"No, I'm saying that because I see the way you are with Autumn and Jacob. You're good with them. You care. And they care about you too. So does Fable. You two have become close. She likes having you around. That's not because someone got you the job. You've *done* a good job. There's a difference."

I'm quiet. I don't know what to say to him, how to answer that. His words make me feel good. Like I've accomplished something. I've just been living these last few months. Surviving. It's been such a confusing time, and while I know so many others out there are suffering way more than I am, I still felt like I was suffering. I also realized I'm selfish.

I am. I can't deny it. I've been that way my entire life. I'm trying to be better, and becoming a nanny — while not my first career choice — has taught me that the world doesn't revolve around me.

"Thank you," I finally say. "I appreciate that."

"Sometimes we need to hear someone tell us we're doing a good job. It can be hard to keep going when no one is there to root for you." He clears his throat and I turn to look at him, noticing the ruddiness in his cheeks. "When you told me you were proud of me earlier, it felt good. I needed that."

His words are achingly sincere and I give in my to urges. I touch his knee, run my hand slowly up so my fingers curve around his thigh. He's warm and firm beneath his jeans, solid and real. This moment isn't fake. It's not.

It's one hundred percent real.

And I don't ever want it to stop.

"I'm sorry I laughed at you earlier." At his confused look, I explain further. "The band thing. It was fun to tease you about it. You looked so offended."

"That's because I *was* offended." His smile is big and aimed right at me. I clutch his thigh tighter, glad I'm sitting because that smile rivals a thousand bright suns and makes me weak. "But I get it. You were embarrassed about your own band geek roots, so it makes you feel better to make fun of others."

"Hey." I smack his thigh, but I swear it hurts my hand more than it hurts him. "Just because you think your drums are superior to my clarinet."

"They are."

"Doesn't mean you can act righteous and tease me about poor band instrument choices," I say primly, removing my hand from his thigh.

He chuckles, the sound rich and warm, making my belly flip with nerves. "You didn't have to stop touching me."

I'm startled he'd mention it. "But—"

"Don't say our relationship is phony. Not right now. This, what we're sharing right now, it's real, Syd." It's his turn to touch me, the back of his fingers drifting across my cheek. I close my eyes, savoring the gentle touch. "You can't deny it. I won't deny it either."

I don't answer him. His words terrify me. It's one thing to think this is real based purely on attraction. I can admit I want to get him naked. What woman wouldn't?

But I also—like him. Spending time alone together like this, we're getting to know each other. Getting closer. Too close.

It's dangerous.

Thirteen
chapter

Wade

I don't want to go home alone. I don't. As we get closer to San Francisco, to Drew and Fable's house, the more I realize I don't want to drop her off, turn around and head back to my place. That sounds awful.

Lonely.

Sad.

Pitiful is what I am. Boo hoo hoo, poor little Wade doesn't want to be all alone with his feelings and his demons keeping him up through the night.

Well, I have no real demons. Shit, I should be on top of the world right now. I should've gone out to a bar when the guys invited me earlier, before I left the locker room. I could've gone out, got drunk, found a girl, and fucked her into oblivion.

But I didn't do any of that. Hell, I couldn't. What if I was somehow photographed with another girl when I'm supposed to be with Sydney? The shit would hit the fan, Drew and Fable would be pissed at me, and Sydney would probably never talk to me ever again.

Not that I wanted to do any of that. Not really. I'd rather be with this girl, right here. Talking to her. Learning more about her. Her revelation was surprising, but then again not. I'm glad she trusted me enough to tell me her secrets. I want to find out more.

A lot more.

And for once, that thought doesn't scare the hell out of me.

Without saying a word, I pull onto an off ramp, which gets Sydney's attention.

"Where are you going?" She sounds confused.

Good. I *am* confused. So at least we can be confused together.

"Can I ask you a question?" I go into the left-hand turn lane and stop at the red light, flicking on my blinker. Ready to turn right around and get onto the freeway headed back to my place if she wants me to.

"Um, sure?"

"Will you come home with me?"

Dead silence is my answer.

Shit.

"Never mind," I mutter, glancing in the rearview mirror, ready to head straight across the street so I can get back onto the freeway and go on to the Callahan house. Dump Sydney off, go along with this pretend relationship plan for the next five days and then call it good.

"No, wait. I didn't say no. Are you—are you sure you want me to come back to your place?" Her voice is a little shaky and

I wonder if she's nervous.

If she is, that's fine. I'm nervous too, not that I'd admit it.

"Only if you want." The light turns green but I haven't turned yet. I don't want to press my luck, or end it. "Only if you're comfortable. We won't do—anything if you don't want to. I just don't…"

"Don't want to be alone tonight?" she finishes for me.

I blow out a harsh breath and nod. "Yeah."

A horn honks behind us and I glance in the rearview mirror again, realizing there are at least three cars waiting to turn. I turn off the blinker, my foot hovering over the gas when Sydney answers me.

"I'll come over," she whispers. "If you want me to."

"I want you to." Before she can second-guess her answer, I hit the gas and turn left, my tires squealing. We're back on the freeway within minutes, both of us quiet, the sexual tension growing with every minute that passes. Or maybe that's just my imagination, but I don't think so. The attraction is there, simmering between us. There's no denying it. I keep sneaking glances at her, anticipation licking through my veins, making me want to touch her.

But I keep my hands firmly locked on the steering wheel.

Sydney's on her phone, sending a text to someone, but I say nothing. Wait for her to volunteer the information instead. "I let Fable know I'm not coming home tonight."

Uh oh. "What did she say?"

"She told me to have fun." She rolls her eyes and starts to laugh softly. "So embarrassing, and kind of weird. I sort of admitted without saying it out loud that I'm spending the night with you."

Does she think I'm bringing her home only to get her in my bed? That's not the case. Not really. Though I'd like to get her in my bed, I won't push...

"I want you to know, I have zero expectations tonight."

"Well, that's kind of insulting." She sounds amused. I hope she is.

"I didn't mean to insult you." Now I'm the one laughing, though not at her. More like at the ridiculousness of the situation. "I just mean, whatever you want to do, I'm up for. If you don't want to do anything, I'm okay with that too."

"Honestly? I don't know what I want. It's not like I plan this sort of thing out, you know? It usually just—happens."

"Same." It's all I can manage to say. Sex is sex. It happens or it doesn't. I never put much thought leading up to it. No expectations, no emotions, none of that. I treat it like a form of release. Sometimes I'm having it with a fun or hot girl, which always makes sex better.

Like Sydney. She's fun. She's hot. The two of us together would probably be pretty damn good.

"A bunch of prep beforehand and candles and silk sheets and rose petals isn't my style," she continues.

"Mine either."

"So you're not a romantic?"

"Not even close," I say, shaking my head. "I'm just a guy."

She's laughing again. "A big, sexy guy."

My head whips to the right, studying her. "You think I'm sexy?"

"Um, yeah." Her tone is pure *duh*, which hey, is flattering.

"You're good-looking and you know it. Plus, you have a lot of muscles."

I keep my gaze fixed straight ahead, ignoring the good-looking comment. Over the years, I've heard plenty from friends and teammates about my pretty face. It's annoying. A detriment most of the time, I swear. "Training all those years gave them to me. I used to be a wimp."

"Right. Well, you're definitely not a wimp now." She slaps her hands over her cheeks, comically embarrassed. "I can't believe we're having this conversation."

"I can't either." I grin, pressing my foot on the gas a little harder. I can't wait to get her home.

We make it back to my apartment in record time, and as we climb out of my truck, I start to worry. I don't have much furniture. A single couch in the living room along with a big screen TV mounted on the wall and my PS4 set up. I have a king-sized bed in the master bedroom and a couple of bar stools at the kitchen counter. That's it, furniture-wise. Hell, I don't even have a dresser in my bedroom. All of my clothes are shoved into the walk-in closet.

I haven't had time to go furniture shopping and I couldn't give a shit about knickknacks and that kind of stuff. Once the season schedule starts in earnest, I won't be around much anyway. I don't need anything beyond the basics for now.

"This is a nice complex," Sydney says as we head down the walkway toward my apartment building. It's dark so she can't see much, but maybe she's just trying to make conversation.

"Thanks. I chose it because it's so close to the stadium. I didn't want to be too far away."

"Smart." She looks around. "It seems very quiet here."

"It's quiet because it's late at night," I tease, and she just rolls her eyes at me in response.

Yeah. She's definitely nervous, not that I can blame her. I glance down at her, trying to fight the warmth that's taking over my chest but failing miserably. There are so many things about this girl…

I like how tiny Sydney is. I like how much bigger I am than her too. Makes me feel like I can take care of her, protect her. Not that she can't take care of herself, but the more time I spend around her, the more I feel almost…caveman around her. Like I want to keep what I think is mine.

Fucking ridiculous, right?

I like her attitude, her personality, how easy she is to talk to, her sparkling blue eyes and her pretty smile. I like how feisty she can be, how honest she's been, how worried she is that I might think less of her because of a couple stupid decisions she's made.

She's young. I've done stupid shit, too. Who am I to judge?

Resting my hand on her lower back, I guide her to my apartment, where I unlock the door and lead her inside. I go to the kitchen and flick on the overhead switch, illuminating the space, and she stands in the middle of my living room, taking in everything.

"It's very…empty," she says when her gaze meets mine.

I shrug. "I haven't had much time for furniture shopping lately. Just went for the essentials."

"Like a PlayStation 4?" She's teasing me again.

"Hey, every guy needs one of those in his life."

"What if I told you I stopped dating a guy because I believed he liked his PS4 more than he liked me?"

"I'd call bullshit."

She raises a brow, silently challenging me.

"Really? He'd rather spend time with his PS4 versus spending time with *you*?" He must've been a total idiot.

Sydney nods, crossing her arms in front of her as she watches me. "He was a total jackass."

"I bet." I go to her, giving in to my need to touch her. Wrapping my arms around her waist, I hold onto her loosely. "I would choose you over my PlayStation 4. Just thought I'd let you know that."

She fakes a surprised gasp as she rests a hand over her chest. "I'm so honored."

"You should be. I love that thing." Bending my head, I brush my lips against hers. She kisses me back, her lips soft and pliant, and I sneak my tongue in for a quick lick before I pull away. "Want something to drink?"

She shakes her head.

"Something to eat?"

"We just ate." She makes an annoyed yet cute face. "How about a tour of your apartment?"

"Okay, though there's not much to see." I throw my arms out wide. "This is the living room."

"No end tables or lamps, huh?"

"Who needs light when you have a big screen TV on?"

She muffles her laughter as I lead her into the kitchen. "Where I cook," I tell her.

"You cook?"

"No. I did find a good Chinese takeout place, though." I turn to meet her gaze. "You like Chinese?"

Sydney nods. "I do."

I'll remember that for later.

I point toward the very small, very empty dining room. "I still need a table, but that's the dining room."

"You do." She pokes my chest, right in between my pecs. "How many bedrooms does this place have?"

"Just one. I wanted something small. I don't need anything big."

I take her down the hallway and point out the bathroom, which, thank Christ, doesn't have my dirty underwear scattered on the floor or dried toothpaste splatters on the mirror. That's been known to happen back in the day when Owen and I lived together, but now that I'm on my own, I try to actually clean up my stuff. Plus, I'm never home to make a huge mess, so that makes life easier.

"And here's where the magic happens," I say as I push open the bedroom door for her.

Sydney peers inside, looking around, and I hit the light switch on the wall so she can see everything better. She quietly takes in my giant king-sized bed that's actually made for once, the black comforter stretched across the mattress with hardly a wrinkle in sight.

"I think you have something against lamps," she says.

I start to laugh. "What's the point when I have overhead lighting?"

She enters my bedroom and turns in a slow circle, checking everything out. "Overhead lighting is harsh and makes everyone look washed out. Haven't you ever heard of mood lighting?"

I decide not to tell her she looks pretty damn good-standing in my bedroom with all that so-called harsh lighting shining down upon her. "Lamps are unnecessary."

"To people who have something against lamps." She rests her hands on her hips. "You don't even have any bedside tables or a dresser."

"So?"

"Where do you plug your phone in at night?"

"On the floor?" She's making a big deal out of nothing.

"Oh, my gosh. You're hopeless." She throws her hands up in the air. "You need someone to take you furniture shopping."

"I don't have time."

"You have two weeks until your first regular season game," she points out.

I'm impressed she knows. "Been learning a little about football, huh?"

"Fable's taught me a thing or two. And I've been paying attention." She points at the closed closet door. "Walk-in closet?"

"Yeah. Don't go in there, though. It's a total disaster."

Sydney

Hmm, spending too much time in Wade's bedroom, staring at that giant bed he sleeps in every night is turning my thoughts into a total disaster. As in, all I want to do is get in that bed with him.

And what would happen afterward would probably end up a total disaster too. I know it. That's why I shouldn't do this.

Taking a deep breath, I turn away from the bed and fix my gaze on Wade. "I like your place." It's bare but definitely has potential. "Add some furniture and a couple of lamps, and you'll be set."

He seriously has something against lamps. There isn't one in this entire apartment. How does the guy see? I hate overhead lights. They're so harsh and most of the time, they make me look awful. All pale and washed out, like a ghost.

"You should come shopping with me." Wade smiles, seemingly bashful, which I find adorable. How can such a big, muscular guy also be adorable? "If you have time. I know Fable has you working extra hard."

"Yeah. She does give me the occasional day off," I tease. "Seriously, though. I'd help if you want me to. Fable would probably love to help, too."

"Just don't pick out anything too girly," he says with a grimace. "I'm not into that look."

"Give me some credit. I wouldn't pink-ify your apartment. I'm not that mean."

"Pink-ify? Good to know." He nods, then glances around, looking as helpless as I suddenly feel.

What next? What, what, what?

"Uh, you want to go watch TV?" he asks.

Is he suggesting we Netflix and chill? I do not want to become a meme. Though I do love Netflix. "Do you actually have cable?"

He shrugs those broad shoulders and I'm suddenly struck

with the urge to climb him like a tree. "I actually don't. I won't be home enough to justify the cost. I do have Netflix, though."

"Do you have a laptop?" When he nods, I keep talking. "Grab it and let's watch something here." I wave a hand toward the bed.

What am I suggesting? I don't want to get in too deep yet I say we should hang out and watch Netflix on his *bed.*

Clearly I've lost my mind.

Both of his eyebrows shoot up. He's super cute when he does that. He's super cute when he does just about anything. "You want to watch Netflix in bed?"

"Yeah, why not?" I glance down at myself. I am completely overdressed for lying in bed watching a movie. "Do you have a T-shirt I can borrow?"

Those eyebrows shoot up again, even farther this time. "Uh, sure. Let me go grab one."

Wade slips inside his walk-in closet and disappears for a bit, finally emerging once more with a MacBook under one arm and a black T-shirt clutched in his other hand. "Here you go. Hope this works."

"Thanks." I make my way to his bathroom and shut the door, turning to face my reflection in the mirror. I look scared. My eyes are extra wide, my cheeks flushed a dark pink and my hair is a little wild. I smooth through it with my fingers then turn on the faucet so I can splash water on my too-hot face.

God, what am I doing? Getting involved with a guy I'm pretending to be with? This is just so strange. But the more time I spend with Wade, the more I like him. That can't be helped. I'm drawn to him. He's sweet and funny and interesting, and the fact that he's incredibly good-looking is just a bonus.

This entire situation is strange. What started out as something awful is quickly turning into something…

Amazing.

Could I get this lucky? Could whatever's happening between Wade and me turn into something real?

Maybe.

Or maybe not.

After I take off my clothes—leaving on my bra and panties, of course—I slip on the giant T-shirt. It falls practically to my knees and the sleeves are so large, they hang to my elbows. I look like the T-shirt is swallowing me whole, but the bonus is when I put my face to it, the fabric smells like Wade.

Yummy.

I exit the bathroom and go into the bedroom to find the overhead light is off and the laptop is sitting open in the middle of the bed, the bright screen casting its glow throughout the large room. The room is otherwise dark, but Wade isn't in here and I'm about to leave in search of him when the closet door opens and he walks out, wearing a pair of black sweatpants and nothing else.

Nothing. Else.

My jaw practically hits the floor.

"I can put on a shirt if you want me to," he starts to say, as if he's afraid he's offending me or something crazy, but I shake my head, needing him to stop whatever it is he's thinking and stay just like he is.

"No. You're fine. Really." I smile, hating how eager I sound. But I can't help it.

I mean, *look* at him.

He is absolute perfection. His shoulders, arms and chest are like a work of art. All I can see is smooth golden skin stretched over defined muscle, his flat stomach ridged—that's a six pack I'm staring at, people—those sweatpants hanging precariously low on his hips.

Oh, this is bad. Dangerous. We're going to sit next to each other on that giant bed, and maybe we're going to snuggle close and then I won't be able to resist. I'll reach out and touch him. I'll probably keep on touching him too, and then I can't be held responsible for what I do next. I might sneak my hand down his pants or something scandalous. And I'm going to guess he won't mind that either. Most guys don't, right?

And look at me, just wearing his T-shirt, silently begging him to touch me, too. I hope he does. Caution is flying out the window tonight, or however that saying goes. Forget it. We only live once. YOLO and all that bullshit.

"Let's pick out a movie," he says, and I eagerly follow him over to the bed, both of us sitting on the edge while he grabs the MacBook and sets it in his lap. He brings up Netflix and we start scrolling through the new movies, our heads bent close to each other's. So close I can smell him, his soapy clean scent like an aphrodisiac to my senses.

I could inhale him all night if he'd let me.

He wants to watch some manly action movie that came out at the very beginning of summer—and is already on Netflix, so that should tell us something—and I readily agree because I don't care. I won't be able to focus on the movie anyway. All I'll want to do is stare at the man lying next to me, looking good enough to eat what with all that skin on display.

We figure out a place to set the laptop and then I fluff the pillows so we can prop our heads up and see the screen. He grabs a throw blanket from the foot of the bed and drapes it over both of us, the laptop propped in between. It's cozy. Intimate. I'm shivering, even though I'm not cold. More like I'm nervous.

Excited.

"Ready to watch?" he asks, his finger poised over the correct key on the laptop.

When I nod, he hits play and the movie starts. But I'm already unfocused, unable to pay attention. I don't care about the movie. I'm too aware of Wade. Every little move he makes, the sound of his breathing, the scent of his skin. How his hair rustles on the pillow when he turns his head, and I want to run my fingers through it. He sniffs and I sneak a glance at him, staring at him unabashedly while he watches the movie.

But he can feel my gaze on him, and finally he turns to look at me, a closed-mouth smile curling his perfect lips. "You hate my movie choice, huh?"

"No, not at all." I try to turn my attention to the laptop screen, but I can't get into it. My eyes travel back to Wade like they can't help themselves, and I find that he's still watching me. That same smile still on his face, his dark eyes warm as they study me. "Okay, fine, yes, I hate it."

"Why didn't you say so?"

"I was trying to be agreeable."

He leans in a little closer, his face practically in mine. "Maybe I don't always like agreeable."

"Seriously?" He must be a liar. All men appreciate agreeable.

At least, the ones I know seem to.

"I kind of like it when you put up a fight."

"What do you mean?" I frown.

"You don't always agree with what I say. And when you were giving me shit about the band thing earlier—I know I was irritated, but I also kind of liked the back and forth with you." He reaches out and brushes a stray strand of hair away from my face.

"So you're saying you like it when we argue."

"Uh huh."

"Even when I disagree with you."

"Well, yeah. I like a challenge." His hand moves down, fingers brushing the side of my neck before he curves them around my nape. "It's more exciting, don't you think?"

What's exciting is lying in his bed with his hands on me. I turn so I'm facing him head on, meeting his gaze for the briefest moment before his drops to focus on my lips. They tingle, like he's literally touching them, and my entire body aches with anticipation. "Shouldn't we be watching the movie?"

"Did you really come here tonight to watch a movie, Sydney?" He arches a brow, the look incredibly sexy, and I'm tempted to throw myself at him.

But I don't. Not yet. The delicious anticipation slipping through my veins as we stare at each other, barely touching each other, tells me this is going to be worth the wait. "Did you really invite me here tonight to watch a movie, Wade?"

His fingers tighten around the back of my neck and he pulls me in closer. So close, our chests bump and I reach out, my fingers brushing against the hot, hard skin of his chest.

Oh my God, this man is going to be the absolute death of me.

"I don't want to watch a movie." He lifts his leg and kicks the laptop shut, the room immediately going dark.

"You should put away your laptop." Could I sound any lamer? What am I, his mom?

"Fuck the laptop." He nudges the laptop off the bed with his foot. I hear it land with a soft thud on the floor and I want to say something. Tell him he's being crazy and neglectful, but I keep my mouth shut.

Not like I can talk anyway, what with the way Wade just pressed his lips to mine.

Chapter
Fourteen

Wade

I close my eyes and sink into Sydney's mouth, tasting her, savoring her, caressing the back of her neck with gentle fingers. The first touch of my mouth on hers lights a spark between us, flaming higher and higher with every stroke of our tongues, every shuddering breath across heated skin, every whispered sigh. She shifts closer to me, both of her hands resting on my chest before she starts sliding her fingers eagerly across my skin, making me shiver. I was hot enough before we started this.

Now I feel like I'm on fucking fire, just from her hands lightly touching my chest.

Wasting no time, my tongue searches her mouth, and I circle her tongue with mine, making her whimper. That needy little sound goes straight to my dick and I tug on her silky hair, tilting her head back so I can deepen the kiss. And she lets me, her head falling back, her lips still locked with mine. Her enthusiasm fuels me, driving me to take more, take harder, take faster, but I remind myself to keep it slow. Keep it easy.

The last thing I want to do is scare her off.

Her hands are everywhere. Wandering. Searching. Along my shoulders, across my collarbone, sliding over my pecs, cruising down along my ribs, my stomach. She's not shy when she touches me. In fact, she's downright greedy as her fingers curl around the waistband of my sweats, her knuckles brushing against sensitive, rarely touched skin, making me quiver.

Making me sweat.

I try to pull away from her touch, but she just grips the top of my sweatpants tighter, refusing to let go. Her fingers slowly slide beneath the fabric, pausing before they go farther, and I hold my breath, waiting for that moment when she makes her discovery. A tiny gasp escapes her and she whips her head up, her surprised gaze meeting mine.

"Um." A pause, and she licks her lips, the sight of her pink tongue driving me out of my mind. I exhale raggedly, trying to grasp onto the tiny threads of control I've pretty much lost, knowing exactly what she's about to say. "Are you wearing any underwear?"

I shake my head. Couldn't she tell from the tent I'm popping that I'm free balling it?

"Oh," she whispers, her fingers drifting straight across my dick. It jerks beneath her touch. "Wow."

Christ, her fingers on me feel good. I shut my eyes, clench my teeth so tight it almost hurts while she continues her exploration. She runs her fingers across my lower belly, just her thumb skimming the length of my erection then back up, which somehow feels erotic as hell. She's hardly touching me, driving me out of my ever-lovin' mind, and I need to make her quit. I haven't been with a woman in months, not since I've started training with the Niners. One wrong move and I'm blowing. If she wraps her fingers around my cock and strokes once, that's gonna be it. It'll be all over.

"Stop, Syd." I grab her wrist, halting her from further exploration. "You're driving me fucking crazy."

She lifts that big blue-eyed gaze back up to mine once more, her parted lips damp and plump and so fucking sexy all I can think about is devouring her. "You really want me to stop?" The doubt in her voice is strong. She has no idea the effect she has on me.

"If you want me to come all over your fingers, then yeah. I suggest you stop," I say gruffly, removing her hand from my pants. "We need to take this slow or it'll be over before it's even started."

"Oh." Her eyes are sparkling and she's smiling so big I swear I can see every one of her teeth. I think she's pleased by what I just said. "I don't mind if that happens."

"Yeah, well, I mind. It's way too soon." Chuckling, I shake my head. I need to regain control of this situation. I didn't want to push for fear she'd ask me to stop, but hell. She took over, and she wasn't shy about it either.

And I have to admit I like it. I didn't think she'd be so pushy, but she's a constant surprise.

Taking control, I grab hold of her and roll over so I'm hovering above her on my knees, her back flat on the mattress, her hips in between my legs. She's just wearing that T-shirt of mine, an old one from college that's thin and soft, and I'm dying to lift the hem. Check out what she's got on under there.

"Am I squashing you?" I ask. I've had women complain I'm too heavy in the past. I'm a big guy, tall and heavy. It wasn't so bad when I was in high school. Hell, when I first started college I wasn't this big either. But the constant weight training has upped my size and now every time I'm with a girl, I'm afraid I'm going to crush her to death.

Sydney slowly shakes her head, her golden blonde hair spread out all over my pillow. I let my gaze roam over her, taking in her every delicate feature. Damn, she's pretty. And she's going to be mine—at least for tonight.

"You feel good," she whispers, her eyes glowing as she smiles up at me.

I kiss her soft and slow, taking my time. Again and again, soft, sweet kisses that linger more with every pass. Until she winds her arms around my neck to keep me close, her fingers diving into my hair and I groan into her mouth. I'm a sucker for someone running their fingers through my hair. I've always loved it. I think that's why I grow it long, which is vain and ridiculous, but there's a bit of truth there. Plus, when it comes to getting haircuts, I'm lazy.

These kisses I'm experiencing with Sydney are lazy too. They're long, tongue-filled, languid kisses where we're exploring each other's mouths like we have all the time in the world, which we do. I don't want to push. We don't need to rush.

And I can't stop kissing her. Tasting her. Enjoying the

sensation of her mouth on mine. I suck on her bottom lip, making her squeal softly. I nibble on that same bottom lip, making her whimper. I lick that lip, catch it between my teeth, suck it, do it all again and again until she's writhing beneath me, restless.

Wanting more.

It's my turn to let my hands wander. I keep my mouth on hers while I touch her. Run my hands down the length of her body until I reach the hem of the T-shirt, then I work my way beneath the fabric, encountering warm, soft skin. I touch the outside of her thighs, her hips, my fingers catching on her thin panties. She sucks in a breath and I move up, my hands still beneath the shirt as they skim along her waist, her ribcage, fingers tracing her delicate, lacy bra.

I glance up to find her head thrown back, eyes closed, her lips parted as she struggles to breathe evenly. She's beautiful like this, lost in my touch, and I grab the hem of the shirt, lifting it up, slowly revealing her.

"Let's take this off," I whisper.

She opens her eyes and sits up, shucking the shirt off in quick, efficient movements, tossing it onto the floor beside the bed. I eat her up with my gaze as she sits before me clad only in the bra and panties. My eyes have adjusted to the darkness and I can see that they're black lace, stark against her skin. Reaching out, I trace one bra strap, then the other, my fingers lingering on her petal-soft skin.

A shuddery breath leaves her and I lean in, dropping a line of kisses along her collarbone. She tilts her head back on a sigh, her hands coming up to clutch at the back of my head, almost as if she wants to guide me to where she wants me next.

It hits me then. What we're doing. How we're about to take a major step. This is serious.

I pull away from her grip, needing the distance for what I'm about to say. Her eyes flash open, full of confusion and she parts her lips, ready to say something. Before she can speak, I rest my index finger over her mouth, silencing her.

"What we're about to do…changes everything." I pause, letting my words sink in. "This was supposed to be fake. What we're doing. But it doesn't feel fake right now."

Fuck. I can't believe I just said that.

She says nothing.

Her silence is deafening.

The silence might be my answer.

Sydney

I don't know what to say. Wade's right—what we're about to do *will* change everything between us. Sex will take this so-called fake relationship straight into the next level. From fake to real after the first orgasm, right? And I want that.

I do.

But I'm also scared. Terrified of what could happen next. What if I end up really liking him? At one point I thought I could keep this strictly physical. After that first kiss in his truck for the cameras, I liked the idea of hooking up with him. He could scratch my itch, fulfill my needs, help ease the loneliness I'd been dealing with since my parents cut me off.

A few days later and here we are, wrapped up in each other, practically naked in his bed, about to have sex, and he means more to me than a mere scratch to my itch. This is crazy. Things like this don't happen that fast, especially for me. I like this guy. I'm attracted to him, but what we're doing also feels so… serious.

Why? I don't get it. I don't get this — *us*.

Wade traces my lips with his index finger, so gentle it's almost as if he doesn't touch me at all. He's waiting for my answer, probably slowly dying inside, and I don't know what to say.

I can't seem to find the right words.

"Tell me to stop and I'll stop," he finally says, his hand dropping away from my mouth. "I'll take you back home. We can forget this ever happened."

That's the last thing I want to do. I can't just forget this night. It's been a whirlwind of emotions, every one of them intense. From happiness to worry to anger to humor to frustration to pure, agonizing want.

That's how I'm feeling right now. I want him. Why should I deny myself? Or Wade? We both want each other. It's foolish to put off the inevitable.

"I don't want you to stop," I whisper, reaching up so I can touch his face, trace his jawline with my fingertips. He's ridiculously good-looking. Like painfully so, with the soulful brown eyes and the lush mouth and that killer jawline that makes me weak every time I look at his face. I rear up and press my mouth to his jaw, circling my arms around his neck, clinging to him.

He wraps one arm around me, his big hand sprawled across my back. When our mouths finally meet, the kiss is hungry.

Urgent. I can feel his erection brush against my belly and I want him. I want him inside me.

But he takes his time, driving me wild with his mouth and hands. He hovers above me, kissing my neck, my chest, slowly taking off my bra so he can touch and kiss my breasts. He sucks first one nipple into his mouth, then the other, turning me into a writhing, desperate mess, and still he won't slip inside me.

Wade shifts lower, kissing my stomach, along the waistband of my panties, his breath fanning across me and making it hard to breathe. He places his hands on the inside of my legs and spreads them wider, his mouth right there, kissing my thighs just before he presses his face against the front of my panties and breathes in deep.

Oh God, I could probably come just from his breaths on my clit. This is insane. Completely, totally, wonderfully insane.

I reach for him with desperate hands, my fingers sliding into his hair, tugging on it. He misreads my silent cues, rising up so his face is in mine once more, and he kisses me. That's okay. I might've wanted him to go down on me, but then again maybe I don't, because this is the first time we're together and that just feels so intimate. Almost too intimate.

So I return his kiss, my hands sliding all over him, pushing at his sweats, wanting them off. I shove and push at them until he takes over, kicking them off and leaving him gloriously naked for me to touch and explore. I don't hold back, stroking his perfect bare butt, his sides, his erection, making him shudder. I circle my fingers around the thick length and start to stroke, but he doesn't let me do that for very long.

"Be right back," he tells me, punctuating the statement with a quick kiss.

Then he slips out of my grip, slips out of bed and disappears.

I lay there, blinking up at the ceiling. What was that about? Where is he going? Without thought I shed my panties, tossing them on the floor, wanting to be as naked as Wade is. He needs to hurry. I'm all anxious and twitchy, dying for his hands on me, his mouth on me, needing him inside me…

"Condoms," he says as he practically runs back into the bedroom. He tosses an entire box on the floor, one wrapped condom still clutched in his hand, and I laugh in relief.

"I thought you bailed on me," I tell him as he crawls into bed with me.

"Hell no. I'm not stupid." But he is warm and big and that skilled mouth of his lands on mine, drugging me, sending me straight out of my mind with every press of his lips, every swipe of his tongue. I lose myself in his kiss, the touch of his hands, the sensation of his big, muscular body wrapped all around mine. He's big and hot, his hands busily roaming all over my body, as if he's trying to memorize my skin with his fingertips.

I moan in desperation when he only pulls away to slip the condom on and then he's back, kissing me again, rolling me over so I'm flat on my back and he's above me, his cock probing at my entrance, eager to get in.

I'm eager to welcome him in.

Wade stops, poised above me, and I can feel his gaze on me. I open my eyes to find him watching me, sweat dotting his forehead, his hair hanging in his face, his dark eyes filled with unmistakable want. My heart is racing and I'm trying to control my breathing when he finally speaks.

"You sure about this?"

I love that he's still asking, even though we've already taken it this far. "I'm sure," I whisper.

"Once this happens, there's no going back." He touches my hair, threads his fingers through it and I close my eyes. His fingers stroking my hair feels so good. Everything about this moment is good. Perfect. Right. "We won't be able to change it. And I don't want you to call this a mistake after it's over."'

Like I would. My eyes pop open to find him still watching me carefully. "I don't want you to say that either," I admit. A trembling breath leaves me when he presses his mouth to my forehead, and I close my eyes again. The onslaught of emotions I'm experiencing in this moment is overwhelming, but in the best possible way.

"You want me?"

I nod.

"Then you have me." He slowly slips inside, filling me completely, and I wrap my arms around him, holding him close, not wanting to let him go. We remain still for a moment, I can feel him pulse deep inside my body, and it hits me that I've never felt more complete.

"I'm yours," I whisper against his neck, just before he starts to move.

"Mine," he whispers back, his deep voice possessive.

He claims me with every thrust, filling me more and more, deeper and deeper. I squirm beneath him, wrap my legs around his hips and anchor my body to his but ne never stops moving. He picks up the pace, pushing faster, rocking against me, his breathing ragged as he pants against my ear. I pull away so our mouths can meet and he devours me, our tongues tangling.

The tingling starts low in my belly, telling me I'm close. My breath starts to catch when he hits a particular spot and I whimper. Oh God, it feels so good. He feels so good. I don't ever want him to stop. I want him to keep on making me his, over and over and over…

"Oh God," I cry just as my orgasm hits me. Tremors race over my body, making me shudder again and again. He comes right after me, a harsh moan rumbling in his chest as he goes completely still for a single, hanging moment. Just before he shudders and shakes, my name falling from his lips.

Hearing him say my name makes my eyes pop open and he lifts his head, his gaze meeting mine, a satisfied smile curling his lips. He kisses me like he can't resist my lips and I return the kiss with equal enthusiasm.

Sex has never felt so right before. Or so perfect. This man is somehow becoming everything to me. And while that's a pretty serious thought, for once, I'm not afraid.

"Let's do that again," he murmurs against my mouth, making me laugh.

I'm not about to protest.

chapter
Fifteen

Wade

I bring Sydney back to Drew and Fable's house the next morning, just before noon. We stayed up most of the night before talking, kissing, laughing, fucking…

Yeah. Lots of that, particularly the last one. We couldn't seem to keep our hands off each other. When we finally woke up and Sydney said she wanted to wash up, I followed her into the bathroom. Where I proceeded to join her in the shower so I could wash her hair, wash her body, then fuck her up against the cool tile wall. She loved every minute of it.

And so did I.

What I especially love is how it's so easy, being with her. She makes me smile. I like her laugh. She's smart. She's interesting. And she drives me out of my mind with lust. One secretive look from her—even when she's not trying to be purposely seductive, I'm a goner—and I'm ready to jump her.

Like right now. She's giving me that one particular secretive look, with the little closed-mouth smile that drives me wild, and I'm contemplating taking her somewhere else, anywhere else. Just so I can be alone with her for a little while longer.

Shit.

I'm getting way too into this fake relationship. Getting way into this too real girl.

We pull into the Callahan driveway, my mood gone to shit when the front door of the house flies open and Fable's running out onto the porch, waving her hand in the air. I roll down the window and hear her shout, "Wade! You need to come inside!"

Shooting Sydney a curious look, I park the car and shut off the engine. "What's going on?"

Sydney shrugs, her gaze skittering away from mine. "I don't know." But she looks suspicious. Like she's in on something.

Huh.

We get out of the car and I follow Sydney to the front door, where Fable is still waiting. She acts like she can barely contain herself, and when the two women share a mysterious look, I know without a doubt they're up to something.

I just wish I knew what.

"Someone's here who wants to see you, Wade," Fable murmurs, taking my hand so she can lead me into the house. After she shuts the door, Sydney follows behind us, and my mind is busy trying to figure out who could possibly be here, wanting to see *me.*

"Who is it?" I ask, knowing my question is futile. They're going to drag this out.

"You'll see," Fable singsongs, looking mighty pleased with

herself. She leads me toward the living room and I glance over my shoulder, sending Sydney a questioning look.

But she just shrugs and offers me an apologetic smile in return.

"What the fuck, dude? I thought you'd show up first thing when you found out I was here," says a familiar voice from behind me.

I turn to find Owen standing in the Callahan living room, a shit-eating grin on his face. Happiness bursts through me and without thought, I throw myself at him, enveloping him in a big hug and squeezing him tight, like I've just been reunited with my long lost lover.

"I didn't even know you were here," I mutter as I pull away from him to stare at his familiar face. He looks good. Older. It's only been a few months since we've locked eyes, but still. "Guess they were surprising me." I send Fable and Sydney an accusatory glare, but they both just smile at me in return.

"Naw, that's my fault. I was just giving you shit. I wanted to surprise you, too. I showed up at their doorstep a couple of hours ago. Fable had no idea this was happening, though I warned Drew me and Chels were coming today."

"Wait a minute. Chelsea's here too?" I glance around the living room, but I don't see her.

"Yeah, she's upstairs with the kids. Autumn was showing her something in her bedroom." Owen shakes his head. "You're a sight for sore eyes, man. Looking good. Looking *tough*. How are those Niners treating you?"

"Pretty damn good. How's Denver?" I ask him, eager to learn everything that he's been doing since he left for Colorado.

"Hey, you two. Come over to the couch and sit down," Fable says, sounding like a meddling mother. But I can forgive her since she put this together just for me. She loves her brother so damn much that she's willing to give up time with him so we can see each other. "Sydney and I will go get Chelsea and us girls will hang out for a bit with the kids. Give you two some alone time to catch up."

"Thanks, Fabes." Owen kisses his sister on the cheek and she gives him a quick hug.

We go to the couch and sit on the opposite ends, the two of us grinning at each other. It's so good to see him in the flesh. I've missed him. After spending so much time together all those years, it's hard to adapt without Owen around. I know he feels the same way.

"Denver's going good. I like it there. Chelsea and I are learning the city and I'm learning the plays, and they're a good team. Solid. I think we're going to kick your ass this season." Owen laughs. "In fact, I can guarantee it."

"Asshole," I mutter, making him laugh harder. "We should bet on that."

"You're on."

We share stories about our respective teams, the players, the coaches. Owen tells me about the new house he and Chelsea bought, how they want to get married soon, probably after the season ends. Then maybe they'll try and start a family, they're not sure yet. His face gets this certain expression, sort of hazy-eyed and dazed, and I know he's still madly in love with her, which is great. It is.

But it's also crazy, seeing him like this. Hearing him talk

like this. I'm sort of blown away by his plans for a house and marriage and a future that includes children, but I know Owen and Chelsea have been on that track for a while now. I shouldn't be shocked.

But maybe it's hitting me harder after what happened with Sydney and I last night—and over these last few days since we started this charade. Being with her like this, seeing her all the time, getting to know her, being *inside* her, has me thinking future thoughts too. Not as serious as what Owen's going through, but it's still overwhelming. I've never contemplated my future with a girl before.

Ever.

"Who's the chick? Well, I know she's Fable's nanny. And that you two are faking a relationship to take the media attention off Drew and the nanny doing the nasty story." Owen shakes his head and I'm in shock. Guess Fable's told him everything. "You two looked pretty serious, though, when you pulled up in your truck."

"What, you were spying on me?" I ask incredulously.

"Maybe. Not on purpose." Owen shrugs. "So what's going on with you and the nanny?"

"We're in a fake relationship, just like you said."

"Right." The skeptical look on Owen's face is obvious. "It didn't look fake, what I just witnessed. You didn't even have an audience."

"I like her," I say simply, not willing to go into more detail. Not yet. "Yeah, it's fake, but I enjoy spending time with her. She's fun. She's sweet. She's beautiful." Just looking into her eyes makes my dick hard and when we kiss? Forget it. All I can think about is taking her clothes off.

Owen is shaking his head. "I can't believe it. Seriously."

"Why? What's the big deal?" I'm getting pissed, which is stupid. But seriously, he can't imagine me in a relationship? What's the problem?

"It's just weird, man, the fake relationship thing. It's exactly how Drew and Fable met, you know? Don't you remember?"

I frown. "Remember what?"

"Those two started out in a fake relationship. One week. He paid her to be his girlfriend for one week over Thanksgiving break when he had to go home to the fam. What a shit show that was. Fable told me all about it. But there was a good thing that came out of it, and it was Fable and Drew falling in love. Only took them a week, and bam—they knew. Now look at them."

I had no freaking idea. "Are you serious right now?"

"Yeah, I'm serious. Come on, I know I told you. I told you everything back then. I still do." He studies me closely. "You don't remember that story?"

Not really. But when you're thirteen, fourteen years old, you're not worried about your best friend's older sister doing crazy shit like that. You'd rather focus on weed and girls and sports. Back then I was completely self-absorbed. "So all it took was a week and they fell in love."

"Yep, that's it. Fable always told me when you know, you know. I never believed it then. I thought those two were a fluke. But then, that's exactly how I felt about Chelsea too. The first time I saw her, it was weird. I just knew that girl would become a big part of my life. And the more time we spent together, the more right it felt."

Damn. Like with me and Sydney. The more time I spend with her, the more I want to be with her always.

It's downright scary.

"So a few days in and you're already feeling it, huh?" Owen grins. "Think the fake relationship is working with the media? Fable says it is."

"Well, I don't know. Sydney had a reporter come up to her yesterday after our last preseason game calling her out on it," I tell him.

"No shit? What did he say?"

"Said something about how he knew we were faking it and our new relationship was a great distraction, but they couldn't be fooled."

"What an asshole," Owen says, shaking his head. "Did you kick his ass?"

"He didn't say that to me, he said it to her. Then he took off. I never even talked to the guy."

"Yeah, because he knew you'd flatten his ass if he said that to you. He's not stupid."

Right. I would've flattened that guy's ass. I wonder if there's anything on the web today about us. I wouldn't doubt it. I'm sure that guy—whoever he was—ran off and posted a false story on the Internet.

The bastard.

"Listen, just keep up the good work and make it look like you can't live without her. Since she just came from spending the night at your house." The smirk Owen sends my way makes me chuckle. "Then you must be doing something right. Maybe you'll finally settle down like the rest of us after all."

"Settle down? Screw that noise." I wave a hand, dismissing his words.

"Screw you, jackass. Let yourself fall for once, you know? There's nothing wrong with having a girlfriend. Trust me. It's nice having someone who loves you unconditionally, who's there for you when you need her." His gaze meets mine, his expression sincere. "It's okay to need someone, Wade. You don't have to do everything by yourself."

I want to believe him. I want to trust what he's saying is true. I want to trust Drew. And Fable too. They all preach the same thing. A steady girl wouldn't hurt me, or my career. She'd keep me straight.

But I'm still wary. Relationships are bullshit. People come, and people go. They rarely stick together. It's a fact of life. So can Sydney and I really be a thing?

I don't know.

Sydney

"I can't believe you're going to have another baby." Chelsea, Owen's girlfriend, fiancée, whatever she is, smiles brightly at Fable as she reaches across the table and grasps Fable's hand, giving it a squeeze. "Are you guys excited? When are you due?"

"More like I'm tired. The baby is due in April." Fable's smile is weak. We're sitting outside on the back patio at one of the tables close to the pool, the giant umbrella above us providing plenty of shade against the warm August sun. "Though yes, we're both excited, and more than a little surprised. This baby was unexpected, and I have to be careful. I don't need any more complications."

Chelsea's expression turns somber. "I remember. That was so frightening, when you were in labor with Jacob."

"Tell me all about it. I don't think Drew can go through that again," Fable says wryly.

I listen to their conversation about babies, covertly studying Chelsea. She's pretty, but not what I pictured Owen's girlfriend to look like. And I don't even know why I'm thinking that, but I guess I had some presumptive thoughts. Besides, I've heard a lot about Owen Maguire since I've started working for the Callahans. I've seen photos, seen videos on YouTube even. He's larger than life, with a charming, magnetic presence that draws people to him.

Chelsea on the other hand, is quiet. I can tell. Her long, dark brown hair is pulled into a side braid and she's not wearing any makeup, though she looks great without it. She has beautiful blue eyes that remind me of the sky and clear, creamy skin. She's wearing a simple black sundress that gently clings to her curves, showing off her tanned arms. Her face is friendly. Open. And that reassures me.

My mind starts to drift, my thoughts filled with grandeur. What if Wade and I can really make this work and have an actual relationship? He and Owen are so close. They make sure they're involved in each other's lives. This means Chelsea and I would most likely have to spend a lot of time together, too. Could we be friends?

I hope so.

"How long are you and Owen here for?" I ask Chelsea.

She smiles at me, revealing straight, perfect teeth. "Only

until Tuesday afternoon. Owen has to get back to practice on Wednesday."

"Aw, that's so soon! I was hoping you guys could stay through the week," Fable says, sounding sad.

"Come on, Fable. You know the drill. You're a football wife." Chelsea sends her a meaningful look. "Besides, I need to get back so I can go to class."

"So you're definitely going to school there?' Fable asks.

"Yeah, I may as well. I need to finish up my master's degree and Owen didn't want me waiting any longer. So I'm enrolled in a couple of classes. I think I can finish everything in the next year if I stay focused, but we'll see," Chelsea explains.

Wow. Her master's degree? I'm impressed. She's smart. And I'm not. Great. We'll probably have nothing in common.

"That sounds like a good idea," Fable says with a nod. "Just don't let Owen distract you, and you'll be fine." They both laugh.

Chelsea turns her gaze on me. "Do you go to college, Sydney?"

I shake my head, suddenly uncomfortable. This is the last thing I want to talk about. "No. Not right now."

Fable frowns with concern. "Oh. Do you want to go? You never told me. You should enroll in a few classes. I'm sure we could work around your schedule."

She's always so nice, so accommodating. I don't know how I lucked out with her as my boss. Even with the naughty nanny drama, I have no regrets. I can't. I met Wade through them and he more than makes up for all the nanny stories.

"I can't really afford to go." There. That sounds like a

perfectly good excuse.

"What do you mean? If you can't afford college, you should look into scholarships. There are a ton of them out there," Chelsea says.

"I probably wouldn't qualify for any of them." When they stare at me blankly my brain scrambles, trying to remember what my high school counselor told me. "Um, I'm still considered a dependent on my parents' taxes, so that's why I don't qualify. They make too much money."

Way too much money, but they don't need to know that tiny fact.

"Ah. I get it." Chelsea nods. "Yeah, that happened to me too, even though my parents weren't contributing anything toward my college fund. Considering they couldn't, since my dad was in jail."

Wait. What? My eyes go wide. Her dad is in jail? I can't believe she just admitted that.

"I'm so sorry." I don't know what else to say.

She shrugs. "He stole millions of dollars from his clients. He deserved to be in jail, though he's out on parole now. Got out early for good behavior. My mom took him back too. I'm sure they're very happy together." The sarcasm in her voice is evident.

"Chelsea doesn't really talk to her parents right now," Fable says to me in a low whisper, making Chelsea laugh, though there's not much humor there.

"Understatement of the year." Chelsea shakes her head, her gaze sympathetic when it lands on me. "Sorry to dump on you the first time we meet. But this is as real as it gets around here with the Maguire-Callahan family."

"No, I get it. I—" My voice falters. "I don't get along that well with my parents right now either."

"You don't?" Fable looks surprised—and concerned. I'm learning this is typical Fable. She's always watching out for others. "Please don't tell me it has to do with all those false stories swirling around you and Drew."

I shake my head. "No, what happened between us was before I came here, though I'm sure they're pissed about the naughty nanny story, too." I hesitate. They're being so truthful with me, so should I do the same? I have nothing to lose here, I guess, except respect. "They're mad at me because I lied to them."

And then I decide to lay it all out. I launch into the story about my senior year, lying about how I got into college, and how my parents caught me in my lies. How they kicked me out of the house and left me on my own.

"How awful," Chelsea murmurs when I finish.

"But look at how well you've done since you've been doing it on your own, Sydney. Maybe it was a good thing, what they did," Fable points out.

I like that she's trying to keep this positive. I can appreciate that. At the time my parents kicked me out, it didn't feel like a good thing. I'd been terrified. Scared I'd fail, afraid I'd have no one to count on.

But now, I'm not scared. I feel…strong. Despite the disaster with the media and all the gossip, I'm with people who want to help me. Who are there for me. I don't think I could say that before, when I was still at home and living a shallow, meaningless life.

In the short time I've worked for the Callahans, I've found some purpose. I've found meaning. I haven't figured everything out yet, but that's okay.

I still have time.

chapter
Sixteen

Sydney

That night, we all go out to dinner, like we're one big cozy family. Which I guess we are, if you look at the main players in the group. The six of us plus the two kids go to a nice family-style seafood restaurant in downtown San Francisco, where we stay for almost three hours, laughing and eating and talking so much, my throat is getting sore. The restaurant is full of tourists who stare goggle-eyed at Drew most of the time, some of them even coming up to ask for his autograph, which he gladly gives them. He takes photos with them too, telling them to get Owen's and Wade's autographs as well, since they're both going to be famous football players someday.

It's nice, to witness Drew so easily include Owen and Wade with the fans. Drew is such a good guy. I respect him more and more as every day passes. I feel the same about Fable.

Same with everyone here at this table tonight.

"You still want to stick with this guy after dealing with us all night?" Owen asks from where he's sitting across the table, pointing at Wade, who's sitting next to me. "He comes with a lot of baggage, you know."

I laugh, sending Wade a quick glance only to discover he's watching me carefully. "You guys don't scare me," I tell Owen.

"Well, we should," he says, lowering his voice like he's about to reveal a juicy secret. "I have so much dirt on that guy. I could tell you stories for hours."

"When we get back to Drew and Fable's, you should tell me a few," I say, making him laugh. "Seriously. I'd love to hear them."

"I don't think so," Wade says, his voice firm, his gaze blazing fire at his best friend. "He doesn't need to reveal all my secrets."

"Really? What about the time you—"

Chelsea clamps her hand over Owen's mouth, effectively silencing him, making everyone else laugh.

"Time for you to keep quiet," Chelsea singsongs before slowly removing her hand from Owen's mouth. Owen glares, seemingly irritated, but then he reaches for her, slinging his arm around her neck so he can pull her in for a lingering kiss.

I look away, blushing. That was almost too intimate to witness.

"He really does know all of my secrets," Wade whispers close to my ear, making me squirm. I swear his lips touched my skin, tickling me.

"Are they that bad?" I turn to meet his gaze, my breath stalling in my lungs when I discover the way he's looking at me. Like he cares.

"Nah. Most of them are typical teenage bullshit." His face turns serious. "Though some of the stuff I did in my past was stupid. Borderline criminal."

"I don't care," I say, wanting to reassure him. "We're all dumb when we're young, right?"

"You still are young." He touches my cheek, his fingers drifting across my skin. "Don't know what you're doing with an old man like me."

I roll my eyes. "You're not an old man. You're three years older than me. Big deal."

"You still have a lot of life to live, though. From nineteen to twenty-one, I was going out almost every night, partying and having fun."

Been there. "Maybe I don't want that." Should I have said that? Screw it. Too late.

He lifts a brow. "What do you want?"

I part my lips, ready to say I want him, when we're interrupted.

"You two look waaaay too serious over there," Owen teases. "Are you boring her already, Knox?"

"Not as much as you're boring me, Maguire," Wade returns.

The two of them have given each other grief all night. It's been nonstop and lots of fun. It's helped me to get to know the two of them even better. Plus, Chelsea and I have talked a lot too. I like her. Despite my earlier worries, we really do have a lot in common. I think we could be friends.

I feel a tap on my shoulder and I turn to find Fable sitting next to me, her expression solemn, her green eyes wide.

"Everything okay?" I ask her.

Fable nods, her smile tremulous. She's warned me she gets emotional when she's pregnant, and I think she's ready to bust into a full on emotional moment right now. "You two are perfect for each other," she says, her voice low. "You and Wade? I knew that would happen."

"You knew what would happen?"

"That you two would be a perfect match. That your fake relationship would turn into something real." Her eyes grow misty. "That's how Drew and I fell in love."

"What?" I frown. She's not making any sense.

"I shouldn't admit this. Hardly anyone knows the truth." She glances across the table, where Drew sits with Jacob in his arms and Autumn pressed against his side. He's talking to Owen, his children hanging all over him like he's a jungle gym, and none of it fazes him. Fable's staring at him like she wants to reach across the table and attack him with her lips.

"What are you talking about?" I am so confused.

"Drew and I. We met when he hired me to pretend to be his girlfriend." At my wide eyes she hurriedly explains more. "Not like I was a prostitute or anything like that. I worked in a bar as a waitress. My mom was addicted to drugs. Owen was only thirteen. I needed money so I could take care of him and the amount Drew offered me sounded like a million dollars at the time. So I said yes. Best decision I ever made."

I'm in shock. Drew really *hired* her to pretend to be his girlfriend? Sounds like something straight out of a movie—or a book. "That's the craziest thing I've ever heard."

"No crazier than what you guys are doing." She grabs hold

of my hands and squeezes them, her gaze boring into mine. "So don't let the craziness fool you into thinking what you and Wade have won't work. It can. It happened to me. And who cares how you two met? It doesn't matter how it all started. What counts is where you end up."

Her words stick with me the rest of the night. I'm floored that she told me such a private detail about her life with Drew. More than anything, I can't help but compare her situation with mine.

Is she right? Does it really matter how we met? She and Drew are proof of that, if her story is true. And why would she lie to me about something like that? Look at how much in love they are. Maybe someday I could have that kind of love, too.

With Wade.

Luckily enough, paparazzi are waiting for us when we exit the restaurant, and all of us pose like one big happy family. There is no denying that Drew and Fable are together. They hang onto each other like they never want to let go, and the way they gaze into each other's eyes…ugh. And swoon.

Wade is perfect too. He wraps his arm around my shoulders and hauls me in close, both of us beaming as the photographers keep taking endless photos. The corners of my mouth start to quiver, I'm smiling so much, and I can't wait for it to be over. We give them a two-minute photo opp before Drew's yelling that's enough, it's time for us to go.

So we do.

I'm quiet when we drive back to Drew and Fable's house. Owen and Chelsea are riding with us, Owen and Wade talking nonstop while I sit in the passenger seat and stare out the window at the city lights as they pass by. My mind is full of outrageous thoughts, all of them dealing with Wade. I want to talk to him. Tell him how I feel, though I'm still a little unsure about that.

I start scrolling through my phone, looking up articles about myself and Wade and the Naughty Nanny story. I stop at one particular article, going completely still when I read what's written.

Some local gossip blog claiming that Drew and I are still together, and Wade is nothing but a distraction from the real story. All the details remind me of that rude reporter who approached me after the game.

Wade suddenly rests his hand on my jean-clad knee. "You're quiet," he murmurs. "What's going on?"

I glance up to meet his gaze. "I think I found the article written by that jerk reporter."

Wade's expression hardens. "What did that asshole say?"

"Nothing much that hasn't already been said." I glance down at my phone screen once more. "It's a local blog."

"With a huge reach?"

"Not really. Not that I can tell."

"Then it's no big deal." He says it so easily I can almost believe him.

"You really think so?"

"If we don't let it bother us, it can't bother us." He smiles. "After all, we know the truth, right?"

His easygoing attitude is the complete opposite of his anger from just a few days ago. And I prefer it. He's right. We shouldn't let it bother us. Who cares?

Besides, we know the truth.

He's still smiling at me. "You had fun tonight?"

I nod. "Definitely."

"Mind if I stick around the house for a while and talk with Owen?"

"Of course, I don't mind. Though I'll probably just go to bed. I'm exhausted." I yawn right after I say that, covering my mouth with my hand.

"Right. I'm pretty tired too." The secret smiles we share have everything to do with the reason why we're so tired. We kept each other up most of last night. And while I'm all for a repeat performance, I really do need to get some sleep. It's back to work with the kids tomorrow and they run me ragged even after a full night's rest.

"Maybe I'll sneak into your room later," Wade says when I don't respond.

"You want to sneak into my bed?"

"Only if you don't mind."

With him, I'd never mind.

Wade

It's past one in the morning before I'm finally headed upstairs to Sydney's room. All the women and children immediately went to bed. Drew joined Owen and me at first, the three of us shooting the shit and talking about football. But after a while, the old man got tired and left us alone so Owen and I could talk. And it was good. I told him everything that had been going on these last couple of months, and he filled me in on his life too.

Not just the general, happy-type stuff, but all the bullshit too. All the hard stuff.

The real stuff.

When I could barely keep my eyes open I realized I needed to get some sleep. Fable had offered me to stay in one of the other guest rooms when we first got back, though she winked at me when she said it. I think she knew I planned on sleeping with Sydney tonight, and that was her way of giving me permission.

Not that anything's going to happen tonight. I'm too damn tired. All I really want to do is sleep.

I sneak into her room just like I told her I would, closing the door softly behind me. I shed my clothes and shoes until I'm in just my underwear, setting my phone on the bedside table just before I pull the covers back and slip into bed with Sydney.

She stirs in her sleep, but otherwise, no response.

Pulling the covers over me, I scoot closer to her, drawn in by her warmth. She's downright hot and so soft. Plus, I don't think she's wearing much, which is a bonus. I slip my arm around her waist and snuggle her close, spooning her from behind. She has on a tank top and a pair of panties. That's it.

All thoughts of sleep fly right out the window, my exhaustion gone. Maybe we can mess around for a little while. I let my hands roam, one cupping her right breast when I feel her shift, her perfect ass brushing against my front, making me hard. She's awake.

"Are you serious right now?" she asks sleepily as she stretches against me.

I slowly circle her nipple with my thumb, feeling it bead tight beneath the fabric of her tank. "Are you too tired?"

"Hmm." Her noncommittal answer gives me hope. I also like the way she's squirming in my arms. She's rousing all my essential parts with every shift of her sexy body. "Are you staying the night with me?" she asks.

"If you're okay with it."

"I'm more than okay with it." A sigh escapes her when I push her hair away from her neck and kiss her nape. "This is a nice way to be woken up."

"I can do more." I slip my hand beneath her shirt so I can caress her, my mouth never leaving her neck. "I can do lots more if you want me to," I murmur against her skin.

"I like it when you touch me."

Without hesitation I slide my other hand down her stomach, teasing the waistband of her underwear before I slip in the front of her panties, seeking her out. She's wet and hot and I sink my fingers in between her legs, pleased when she spreads her thighs wider to give me easier access. "So wet," I whisper.

"Oh, God," she chokes out when I start to stroke her silky flesh. A shuddery breath escapes her and she reaches up, winding her arms around the back of my neck, one hand sinking into my hair. The position thrusts her chest out and I tug on her tank top, lifting it up so it curls just above her breasts, exposing her completely. I pluck her nipple and stroke her pussy, my erect cock nudging her ass as I try my best to get her off as fast as possible.

She whispers my name and I increase my pace. I'm eager to make her come so I can get inside her.

"You have condoms?" I ask, my breath ragged.

Sydney shakes her head frantically. "No," she practically

wails.

"Pretty sure I have one in my wallet." I kiss her neck again, just before I sink my teeth into her flesh as I strum her clit. She thrusts her hips up, seeking my touch, and her entire body goes tight as she strains toward her orgasm.

She's so damn close. I can already tell, can already read the signs. I start to whisper in her ear, something filthy, a little something to help her let go and then she's a shuddering mess in my arms, my name falling from her lips, her body quivering as her orgasm sweeps over her completely.

I climb out of bed while she recovers and dig the single condom out of my wallet. Then I'm tearing off my underwear, tearing into the condom wrapper and suiting up before I slip back into Sydney's bed. I don't even hesitate. She's sprawled across the bed as if she was waiting for me and I sink into her welcoming body, my mouth finding hers so I can kiss her into oblivion as I start to move.

The bed creaks with my every thrust. I try to slow down, try to remain quiet, but it's no use. I want her too much. I need her too much. I move faster, her legs wrapping around my hips as she clings to me, our mouths fused together. I can't get enough of her. I wish I could say that out loud, but it's too fast. Too fast. Everything's happening way too fast.

And I don't ever want it to stop.

chapter
Seventeen

Sydney

The phone starts ringing way too early in the morning, before the sun has even risen. At first, I think it's my phone and I blindly reach toward my bedside table to answer it.

But I realize quick just by the texture of the case that it's not my phone. It's Wade's. And the name flashing across the screen says "Mom".

"Wade." I nudge his shoulder and he grunts but otherwise doesn't respond. I poke him again, harder this time, saying his name louder too, and he rolls over, an irritable look on his face as he glares at me.

"What?"

What a grump. I hold the phone out to him. "Your mom is calling."

"Shit," he mutters as he takes the phone, sitting up so he can answer the call. "Hey. You okay?"

He remains quiet and I can hear a panicked female voice on the other end, talking quickly. I clutch the comforter close to my chest, uncomfortable at the thought that Wade is on the phone with his mom while naked in bed with me. After we just had sex a few hours ago. It's kind of weird. But I tell myself to be a grown up and get over it.

"So you're at the hospital? Jesus, Mom, are you okay?"

My heart drops when I hear his words and I sit up, wanting to touch him but unsure if he wants my comfort. What happened to his mother? Is she all right?

I can hear her talk once again, and she's slower now, not so frantic. I listen to her before I start speaking again, trying my best to reassure her. "I'll be there as soon as I can, okay? Yeah. Just—stay there. Don't let them release you. They wouldn't do that yet, would they?"

He pauses, letting her talk before he resumes. "They think you broke your hip, Mom. No, they better not release you, or there will be hell to pay. Just sit tight. I'll be there soon, all right? Bye. Love you." He ends the call then practically leaps out of bed.

"What happened to your mom?" I ask as I sit up, watching as he goes in search of his clothes.

"She got into a car accident. She had the early shift at work and was driving there when some jackass plowed through a stoplight and T-boned her car." He slips on his jeans without his underwear, and even in his moment of panic and fear, I can't help but think he's totally sexy.

Which means I have issues, right? Right.

"Is she okay?"

"She's talking and coherent, so that's good. They think she might've broken her hip. I hope it's not that serious, but we'll see." He slips his shirt on, then looks over at me. "I have to go be with her."

"Yes, of course you do." But how far away is she? "Where is she at?"

"Still in Chico. I have to go home." He sits on the edge of the bed, his heavy weight making the mattress groan and sag, and starts to put on his shoes. "I hate leaving right now with Owen and Chelsea still here, but I have to go."

"They'll understand." I throw the covers back and crawl over to him, slipping my arms around him from behind. "Are you okay?" I whisper close to his ear. He smells so good. Feels good too. So solid and comforting and warm. I wish he didn't have to leave. I hope his mom is okay.

"Yeah. It's just—the timing sucks." He blows out a harsh breath and leans against me, as if he needs my support. Turning his head, his gaze meets mine. "If she's as bad as she says she might be, she's going to need twenty-four hour care for a while."

I squeeze him gently, pressing my body full against his. I'm still naked, but I don't care. I just want to make him feel better. "Maybe it's not as bad as they all think."

"I hope not." He closes his eyes, leaning his head on my shoulder. "I need to be with my mom, but I don't want to leave you."

My heart feels like it just tripped over itself. "You have to take care of her. She comes first, and I understand." I do, I swear. It just—hurts, knowing that he has to leave, and I can't go with him.

"I don't know how long this is going to take."

"Of course you don't." He lifts his head and I pull away slightly so I can start rubbing his shoulders. "But you need to be there for her."

"I have to leave. Right now. The drive is at least four hours." He hangs his head. "God, that feels good."

I rub harder, trying to work out all the knots I can feel in his muscles. "When you come back, I'll give you a full body massage."

Wade glances at me over his shoulder, his expression hopeful, though I can see the exhaustion around his eyes. "Promise?"

"Promise." I lean in and kiss him softly on the lips. When I try to pull away though, he follows, kissing me again. And again. Until his tongue is in my mouth and I somehow end up in his lap, his hands gripping my butt, my naked body wound all around him.

The kiss spirals out of control fast, until I'm basically gyrating on him and his hands are everywhere, his erection straining against his jeans. I know this isn't the time, but maybe a quickie would be good. One last moment together before he's gone for days, maybe even weeks.

God, I'll miss him. I don't want him to leave me ever.

"I don't have another condom," he says minutes later, between ragged breaths, and I sag against him, the disappointment washing over me in thick, heavy waves. We can't do anything. We shouldn't do anything. He needs to leave. Now. "*Fuck.*"

Frustration vibrates off his big body and I crawl off his lap, diving back under the covers and pulling them up to my chin. My entire body is tingling, primed and ready for action, and I watch as Wade rises to his feet, running a hand through his messy hair before he turns to look at me.

"Text me when you get there, okay?"

"I will." He nods, his expression pained, his gaze haunted. "You won't forget me when I'm gone?"

Like that's even possible. "Never." I pause, the question hanging on the tip of my tongue. Screw it. I'm asking him. "We'll still be good when you come back though, right?"

"What do you mean?" He frowns.

"This. What we have. When you come back from taking care of your mom? Or will we miss the expiration date?"

I wait nervously for his answer. We have that one-week deadline Fable and Drew set for us. Is Wade still following it too?

"Forget the expiration date," he says.

"Really?" I sound hopeful — maybe even desperate.

"Yeah. We don't have an expiration date." He comes to me, bending down to give me a fierce kiss on the lips. "I'll be back soon. Okay?"

"Okay." I nod, pressing my lips together.

"I mean it."

I nod again, because I'm too scared to talk. Afraid I might burst into tears instead.

"This is more than a fake one week relationship. You understand that, right, Sydney?" His voice is stern, as is his expression. He means business.

"I do. It's the same for me."

"Good." He kisses me again.

And then he's gone.

That's when I let go and cry.

Wade

It actually takes me five hours to get back to my hometown. Traffic was shit—stop and go—all the way out of the Bay Area, even up to Sacramento, but once I hit Interstate 5 and then Highway 99, it was all clear. I let my lead foot take over and went over the speed limit all the way, trying my damnedest to make up for all that lost time.

I can't stop worrying about my mom, all alone at the hospital and waiting for me to come be with her. It tears me up, imagining my mom injured and unable to take care of herself. She's the strongest woman I know, next to Fable. My mom was always there for me, no matter what.

The one time she needs me the most, and I'm not there for her.

To distract myself, I focus on Sydney. How she's imprinted herself all over me. Hell, after that crazed kiss earlier before I left her room, I can smell her. I *still* smell her, her scent clinging to my clothes, lingering in my head.

If I didn't know any better, I'd guess I was halfway in love with her.

She's the one thing that keeps me focused, keeps me pressing on. I don't know why. I should be focused solely on my mother, but I'm not. And that's okay. Someone else has come into my life now. Someone who is becoming important to me at an accelerated pace.

For once in my life, I'm not inclined to stop it.

By the time I roll into the hospital parking lot, I'm exhausted, hungry and grumpy as shit. I need to find my mom and make sure she's okay, then grab something to eat.

Luckily enough the nurses are patient with me and helpful, and I find my mom's room number with relative ease. I hesitantly knock and then walk into her room, mentally preparing myself for what she might look like. She just went through a car accident. I'm going to guess she's pretty banged up.

And she is.

She's propped up in bed sleeping, her head wrapped in gauze, with two black eyes and a nasty scrape on her cheek. She's completely still, almost too still, and seeing her like this freaks me out, though I try to remain composed. But I guess she has a mom's sixth sense or whatever because her eyes pop open within moments of me arriving, and she slowly turns her head to see me standing there, unsure and feeling scared like I'm a little kid.

"Wade." She tries to smile, but it looks like it hurts her to move, so she quits. "Come here."

I approach her bed slowly, afraid to touch her, afraid to even look at her. "You okay, Mom?"

"Just sore. Very sore." She nods, winces and closes her eyes. "I feel like I've been run over."

"You sort of were." I touch her arm gently, just to make contact. She's warm and smells the same, some perfume she's been wearing since forever. "Did the guy who did this to you get hurt?"

"Yes. He's in the hospital too. I hear his injuries are more severe than mine." She shakes her head. "Such a terrible accident."

"Was he drunk?" I'm angry just thinking about it. He better hope he wasn't drunk. I might want to go kick his ass.

"I don't know. I'm sure we'll find out more details later." She remains still, her eyes remaining closed, the grimace on her face. "I have good news. The doctor says I didn't break my hip. I just dislocated it."

Relief floods me. "That's good, right?"

"It is good, but I fractured my ankle. So that's bad. I'm going to have to wear a cast for the next six to eight weeks."

"Which ankle?" Not that it matters, I guess, I'm just curious.

"The left one."

"Still better than a broken hip," I point out.

"True. But I wish I'd never been in this accident at all." She cracks open her eyes and her smile is strained. "But I can't change it, so I'll just have to deal."

"What about your head?"

"What about it?"

"It's wrapped up like a mummy's."

"Oh. I banged it up. I'm all banged up. I hear I have a couple of shiners."

"That you do." I don't want to tell her how bad she looks, so I keep my opinion to myself. "How long are they keeping you in the hospital?"

"Just overnight for observation. They want to make sure I have no internal bleeding." Hearing those words strikes fear in my heart, and she must see it written all over my face. "They don't think that'll be a problem, but it's a precautionary thing. I'll be here for twenty-four hours, then they'll release me."

"I came as soon as I could. Got caught in the morning commute, so the traffic was hell," I tell her as I find a chair and pull it up to the side of her bed.

"You're so far now, though I guess I shouldn't complain. At least you're not in Denver." She's referring to Owen, which reminds me…

"I saw him. Owen. And Chelsea. They came to visit Fable and Drew for the next few days. They got here yesterday."

"Aw, is he still there?"

"Yeah. But I needed to leave and come see you." I take her hand and hold it loosely, running my index finger over hers. The same familiar ring is on her middle finger, one that my grandma gave her when she turned sixteen. There's another on her ring finger, though, one I don't recognize. It's new and beautiful, with a red center stone surrounded by tiny diamonds.

It looks expensive. Who could that be from?

I won't question her now. Instead, I study her hand, which is slender and dry, a little more wrinkled than the last time I really paid attention to her. I've missed her. Been so wrapped up in my own world that I've neglected her, even those last two years at college when we were living in the same damn town, I didn't talk to her much. Too caught up in my own life to worry about hers, I guess.

Well, that changes now.

"I'm so glad you came to see me, Wade. It does my heart good to look at your pretty face. I've missed it." I roll my eyes at her mentioning my pretty face. She's as bad as my friends. "But you don't have to stay the night or anything. I'll be fine."

Wait. "What? Why do you say that?" My gaze meets hers, confusion slipping through me.

"I've been keeping secrets from you, son, and I'm sorry." She sighs then makes a face, like it hurt her. "I've been seeing someone."

"You have?"

She nods. "Yes. He's a real nice man. He works at the bank I go to. When I went in there over a fraud case and had to get a new debit card, he was the one who helped me. We started flirting and before I left with my new card, he asked me out for coffee."

I'm in shock. "When did this happen?" I vaguely remember her telling me about a debit card issue, but that feels like a long time ago.

"Almost two years ago."

"*What?* Are you serious?"

"Yes. Richard is very nice. I think you'll like him."

"But why didn't you tell me about him?" I'm kind of hurt. Scratch that—I'm *really* hurt. Why did she keep this from me? And for two years? That's a long-ass time. It makes no sense.

"Well, at first I didn't think it would go anywhere, so why bother bringing him into our lives, you know? Let alone mentioning him. We were just friends, but then it grew into something more and now…now we're in love. And a few weeks ago, he asked me to marry him."

"What?" I keep saying that word, but she keeps dropping these bombs on me, so I can't help it. That's where the ring came from. It's an engagement ring.

Holy shit.

"Yes. Married. We're just engaged, so there's no rush. And now with the accident, I'm sure I'll have to wait a little longer. But that's okay. We have all the time in the world."

This time, the smile on her face is real, and I don't think it's hurting her either. She looks content. Happy even. Despite her being banged up and in the hospital with two black eyes and a broken ankle, I can feel the happiness radiating from her.

And it makes me happy too, despite her secret-keeping.

"I wish you would've told me about him," I say quietly. "Why didn't you?"

"I don't know." She shrugs, then winces. "I didn't want to get my hopes up. I've never had the best luck with men. Then after a while, when I realized it was real, you were so busy, I didn't know how to tell you."

"You should've just…told me."

"I know. And I'm sorry."

"You don't need to apologize. Just—don't keep secrets, okay?"

"Ah, well. We all have secrets, though, don't we? Like your new girlfriend? The Naughty Nanny?" Mom teases.

Great. I knew she'd hear about it. Why wouldn't she? Everyone in the world knows, I swear. "Sydney didn't have an affair with Drew."

"Oh, I know. I'm just teasing. Drew is too good to his wife to ever do something like that." She hesitates, her voice going softer. "Is she a nice girl, Wade? This Sydney? Do you like her a lot?"

I'm tempted to tell her the relationship is bogus, but something holds me back. That tiny detail might worry my mom. Or make her ask too many questions I don't want to answer.

Then I think of Sydney naked in her bed this morning. I think of how she hugged me and rubbed my shoulders and kissed me like she meant it. I think of all those things that make her who she is, and how I like every single one of those little details.

"Yeah. I like her a lot. I think you would too."

"You need to bring her over then, so I can meet her, and you can show her your hometown. Then you two can meet Richard."

"You sure you don't want me to wait two years first?" I ask sarcastically.

"Smartass," she mutters, shaking her head, making me grin. She sounds like her regular self, and that reassures me. "Maybe in a few weeks we can come watch one of your games, if I'm feeling better."

"Whenever you want tickets, Mom, I'll put some aside for you. And whatever money you might need too, I'm here. If things go well this season, you might be able to retire by the end of next year."

That's my goal. I want to take care of her so she never has to work again. She's done so much for me my entire life. Now it's my turn to do something for her. It's the least I can do for all the sacrifices she's made over the years.

"Ah, wouldn't that be lovely? I hope it comes true. Then when Richard retires, we could travel the world." She smiles as she closes her eyes. "Thank you for running to my rescue, Wade. It is so good to see you."

"I'm not going anywhere," I tell her. "I'll stay with you here as long as you need me."

"Until Richard's off from work, maybe?"

"Sure you want me to meet him?"

"You're not going to let that go, are you?" she mutters. "Yes. I want you to meet him."

"Then I'll stay here as long as you need me. Is Richard taking you home from the hospital?" I ask.

"Yes. He'll take care of me these next few weeks. Already said he'll take vacation time if I need him to." She grabs hold of my hand again, giving it a squeeze. "He's one of the good ones, Wade. Took me a while, but I finally lucked out and found one. I hope your Sydney is like that. Because once you find a good one, you don't ever let them go. Trust me."

"I don't plan on letting this one go, Mom." I squeeze her hand in return. "I promise."

And I mean it.

chapter Eighteen

Sydney

Couples surround me, yet I'm all alone.

And it totally sucks.

It's been a lazy Monday, the kind where nothing gets done and no one minds. None of us ever left the house, which made watching the kids a lot easier. They were quiet most of the day, and so was I, because I'm still so tired, I feel like a zombie, shuffling around this giant house all day.

We just ate dinner and we're all spending time in the family room before Autumn and Jacob go to bed, watching a kids' movie on the big screen TV. Owen and Chelsea are cozy as they cuddle on the couch, a thick blanket thrown over both of them. Drew and Fable are stretched out on the other couch, Fable leaning against her husband, Drew's arm wrapped around her shoulders. Even Autumn and Jacob have each other. They're sitting on a blanket on the floor, the two of them actually being quiet for once as they watch the movie with rapt attention. Everyone has someone else, leaving me completely out of the equation.

I'm stuck in an overstuffed chair by myself, and absolutely miserable. I miss Wade so much it hurts, which is ridiculous, but I can't help it. He hasn't even been gone twenty-four hours — he only left early this morning, and I'm acting like a pouty baby who didn't get her way. Imagine how I'll be if we're still together and he starts traveling for out of town games.

A straight up mess, I'm sure.

But yeah, that's me assuming we'll still be together. I don't know if that's going to happen. Now with him gone and me having much time on my hands today, I can't stop evaluating our relationship and how it started out as totally fake. Can we really turn what we have into something real? Does he want to? Do *I* want to? The questions keep running through my head over and over, to the point where I'm doubting myself, along with Wade.

I can't deny we have an attraction. Chemistry. Whatever you want to call it. Yes, we had sex. But lots of people have casual sex and then never actually get together all the time. This could happen between us. That's the way it should happen. It makes more sense than us falling in love and living together, happily ever after.

Of course, look what Fable told me last night. She and Drew started out practically the same way. And when I think about their relationship, and how solid and passionate and perfect it seems, I'm blown away. They were forced to spend time together, yet they still fell in love.

Maybe there's hope for Wade and me yet.

Or maybe I'm reading too much into this. Maybe he's going to reject me and I'm going to end up looking like a fool.

My heart hurts just thinking about it. And so does my head. I can't take it anymore.

"Do you mind if I go to bed?" I aim my question at Drew and Fable.

Fable sits up, turning to look at me, her expression full of concern. "Are you feeling okay?"

"Yeah." I nod. "I'm just tired." Not a lie. I'm worn out from Wade keeping me up the last two nights.

"Missing a certain someone?" The knowing smile Fable shoots my way makes me want to throw a couch pillow at her.

But I don't. Because, you know, I want to keep my job.

"Yeah." I shrug, feeling awkward. "Do you want me to put the kids to bed?"

"No, I'll take care of them after the movie's over. Thanks, Syd. Good night," Fable says cheerily.

I stand and they all say goodnight to me, Autumn and Jacob running toward me to give me a quick hug and kiss before they resume sitting on the floor to finish their movie.

I leave the family room and wander toward the staircase. A flash of light suddenly appears through the mottled glass of the front door and I pause, wondering if someone has pulled up to the house.

Weird. Usually they get a call from the gate, unless whoever it is knows the password.

I'm about to head up the stairs when there's a soft knock on the door. Frowning, I approach the door, checking through the peephole to see who's on the other side.

And when I see who it is, I unlock and throw open the door so fast I'm breathless. "What are you doing here?"

Wade stands in front of me, his hands shoved in his rumpled jeans, his T-shirt wrinkled, his hair a mess, his face full of exhaustion. "I heard there's a girl here who'll give me a full body message. I'm hoping to collect payment."

I don't even bother containing my emotions. I throw myself at him, wrapping my arms around him tightly, closing my eyes to fight off the tears that threaten. I'm an emotional mess just seeing him, and I can't explain why. I'm just so glad he's back.

"I can't believe you came back so soon. How's your mom?" I ask, my voice muffled against his chest.

He runs a hand over my hair, then presses his lips to my forehead. "I can tell you all about it, but I'm hoping you'll let me take a shower first?"

My poor, tired, dirty man. I pull away from him, grab his hand and lead him up the stairs, my entire body shaking. He's here. I can't believe he didn't go straight home, that he came over to be with me instead.

I'm so glad he's here. So happy he chose me first.

I direct Wade to my shower and make sure he has a clean towel and washcloth. Then I go ask Drew if he has some clothes to spare for him. Fable helps me dig up a pair of old, ugly red Niners sweats and a T-shirt, a knowing smile on her face the entire time.

"He came for you," Fable whispers just as she hands me the clothes. "It's a sign."

"A sign of what?" I frown.

"That he cares about you. He was thinking about you. He had to come and see you first." Her knowing smile grows even bigger. "You matter to him, Sydney. Don't forget that."

I matter to him.

Those words are on repeat in my brain as I drift back into my bedroom as if in a daze. I knock on the attached bathroom's closed door and then open it, setting the clothes on the counter. I can see him through the shower's glass door, his very muscular, very naked body covered in soap.

The stuff of fantasies, I swear.

I slam the bathroom door shut and then frantically change out of my clothes, throwing on an old T-shirt I wear to sleep and kicking off my shorts so I'm only in my pink cotton panties. Then I dive beneath the bedcovers and wait, the anticipation nearly killing me.

Ten minutes later the door finally opens, steam billowing out of the bathroom. I anxiously wait for him to appear and I sit up, holding my breath as I wait for him to make his appearance. When he finally walks out of the bathroom, I gasp.

And then I immediately start to laugh.

Wade

"What?" I glance down at myself, knowing that she's laughing at the stupid sweats I'm wearing. First, they're too tight. I'm bigger than Drew. Second, they're bright red. Fire engine red. Niners red.

They're kind of hideous.

"I knew those sweats would be ridiculous," she says

between giggles.

I grin at her. "You're mean."

"I can't help it." She starts giggling harder. "Red is not your color."

"They don't even fit me." I walk toward the bed, grimacing as the fabric binds and stretches tight against my boys. I'm kicking these fuckers off as soon as I get in that bed with her, I swear.

Sydney flips the covers back, patting the empty side next to her. "Join me?"

"Gladly." I practically collapse onto the mattress, closing my eyes as she pulls the blankets over me. I can hear her lean over, the click of the lamp as she shuts it off, shrouding the room in darkness.

I crack open my eyes to find her watching me, a silly smile still on her face. "See? Lamps are nice."

"You with the lamp thing again," I grumble, reaching out to grab her and pull her toward me. She comes willingly, snuggling close with her head on my shoulder, and she sighs.

I sigh too. I've never felt so content.

"Tell me about your mom," she whispers.

I give her the rundown. About the accident, how I stayed at the hospital all day until her boyfriend showed up. What a nice guy he is, and how he's not actually her boyfriend but her fiancé. I spilled my guts, telling Sydney everything, and when I finish she lifts her head, smiling drowsily at me.

"You're a good son."

"I guess. Not good enough for her to tell me about her fiancé, though." That still bothers me. I want my mom to be honest with me and not have any secrets between us.

"You're busy. She's busy." Sydney frowns. "Maybe she was worried about how you'd react."

Maybe. I don't know. I guess I kept my mom on a pedestal for so long, it's hard for me to deal when she makes a mistake. "Not sure why, but whatever. It makes me feel bad. I don't want us keeping secrets from each other, and I told her that." I meet Sydney's gaze. "I don't want us to have any secrets either."

"Did you tell her about me?"

"I did."

"Did you tell her the entire story?" She lifts a delicate brow.

"No." Shit. I'm talking out both sides of my mouth here. I tell my mom no more secrets, yet I keep the truth from her. But I couldn't bring myself to tell my mother *everything*. What if she thought differently of Sydney because of our situation? I couldn't have it. "Why worry her or make her wonder what we're doing can't work?" I hold my breath, waiting for her answer.

"You're keeping a secret from her though."

A ragged sigh escapes me. *Busted.* "I know." I pause. "Do you want me to tell her the truth?"

"You probably should." She hesitates. "Eventually. It's the right thing to do."

Yeah. She's right.

"Do you want what's happening between us to work?" Now Sydney sounds nervous. Really nervous.

I need to reassure her.

Reaching out, I touch her face, then trace her lips. "Yeah."

Her smile grows. "Me too."

"Forget the fake shit." I've always been wary of relationships, always keeping it casual, playing it safe.

Until Sydney. Forget casual. She makes me feel safe.

She makes me feel so much, it's hard to describe.

"I agree," she says. "This is for real."

"For realz?" It's my turn to tease and I can't help myself, I start chuckling.

"For realzies." She rears up and kisses me on the lips, a soft, sweet kiss that tells me exactly how she feels about me. "We should take those sweats off."

"I'm wearing nothing underneath them," I warn her.

"Even better," she whispers just before I kiss her again. "Are you wanting to collect on that full body massage now?"

"I don't think so. Not tonight." Another kiss, this one with tongue. "I'll save that for another time. But I am wanting to collect something from you."

"What exactly are you looking for?" she asks.

"You." I kiss her. "Naked." Kiss her again. "Beneath me." One more kiss, with lots of tongue this time, until we're both breathless and panting and her shirt is shoved up over her breasts and I'm cupping them in my hands. "Me inside you."

"That sounds good," she whispers.

"No," I tell her just before I start to kiss her all over again. "That sounds fucking perfect."

Epilogue

Sydney

"I still can't believe you agreed to have all of these people over on Christmas Eve," I tell Fable with a slight shake of my head. We're standing in the formal dining room, the long table covered with a variety of delicious food that smells amazing, despite the fact that I've eaten enough to cover my calorie intake for the next five days. Or more like five years.

Oh well, who's counting?

The Callahan house is jam packed with people, there's Christmas music playing in the background and Autumn and Jacob are running all over the house like savages, the both of them beyond excited at the prospect that Santa Claus is coming tonight.

"Well, you've been by my side helping me with all the planning so no big deal, right?" Fable smiles and rubs her belly, her face glowing. This pregnancy has agreed with her and luckily enough has given her no complications. She looks beautiful in a flowing red dress, and she's still tiny save for the slope of her belly. "Now go mingle. I'm going to go talk to your brother."

My mouth drops open. Gabe and his girlfriend Lucy came to the party, and for some reason, Fable and Gabe have really hit it off. "Seriously?" I guess I shouldn't be shocked. Gabe can be quite charming when he wants to be.

"Seriously. He's funny. So are his friends. I particularly like Shep," Fable says with a smile because yes, Shep and his girlfriend Jade are here too.

"I like Shep, but I've always been partial to Tristan." It's true, even though Tristan has been a total dickwad most of his life, he was always nice to me. His girlfriend Alex has really helped him learn how to not be a dickwad to everyone, which is a bonus.

"Oh, I like Tristan too, and his girlfriend Alex. I love her! Steven and Kelli are sweet too, I'm so glad they brought them." Fable beams. "I love all your brother's friends. They're so much fun." And with that, Fable leaves, calling out Gabe's name when she spots him.

Shaking my head, I go and grab a glass of champagne and sip from it, smiling as I watch everyone talk and laugh. There's a real hodge podge of people here tonight. I invited my brother and Lucy, and he ends up bringing an entourage, which thankfully Fable and Drew don't mind.

I'm just thankful I can surround myself with people I know and love during the holiday season. My relationship with my parents still isn't perfect, but we're slowly healing. Mom and I talk on the phone on occasion. Dad and I chatted on Face Time last week. We're trying, and that's all I can ask for.

"Hey Syd." An offensive lineman for the Niners smiles and nods at me as we walk past each other and I say hi in return, marveling yet again at my surreal life. A year ago—heck, even a few months ago—I would've never believed it if someone told me I'd work as a nanny for a famous NFL player and his wife.

But here I am, working for a wonderful family, looking forward to the newest edition coming soon. Thankfully the paparazzi have moved on, and I'm not referred to as the 'Naughty Nanny' any longer.

Nope, now I'm referred to as Wade Knox's girlfriend, and I don't have a problem with that. Not at all.

I go in search of Wade, stopping to chat briefly with Fable's former boss Colin and his wife, Jen. They own multiple restaurants on the west coast and they are so stunningly beautiful together, it's hard for me to not stare at them. Totally ridiculous, I know, but I'm star struck—by pretty much everyone in this house.

It's when I'm wandering aimlessly through the house a few minutes later that Wade finds me. Strong arms wrap around my waist from behind as he pulls me close to him.

"I've been looking for you," he murmurs near my ear just before he kisses it, making me shiver.

I turn in his embrace, slipping my arms around his neck so I can play with the hair at his nape. "I've been here all night. Where'd you disappear off to?"

"I was with Owen. We were talking." I adore his best friend, and they don't get to spend much time together considering they're both so busy. When they have the opportunity to talk, I don't want to interfere.

"I thought so." I run my hand across his shoulder, down his chest. "You look nice. I like the sweater." It's charcoal gray and extra soft.

"Thanks. I like your dress." It's dark green and also extra soft. His hand slides down my side, then back up, making my skirt rise. I slap at his hand, making him chuckle. "I've always been a fan of dresses."

"More like you're a fan of easy access," I retort, though I'm not angry. Not in the least.

With Wade, I've become a fan of easy access too.

"Quit complaining." He kisses me before I can say something, stealing all my words, my thoughts, with a mere brush of his lips. "Are you having fun?" he asks once the kiss is over.

I nod and snuggle close, his arms tightening around me. "This is the best Christmas I've ever had."

"Really?" He sounds surprised.

"Really." I kiss him this time, rising up on my tiptoes to put my all into it. And I am. The both of us are, the kiss getting deeper and deeper, until I hear a tiny giggle at our feet.

I break away to see Autumn gaping up at us, her hand going over her mouth to contain her laughter. She's wearing a black velvet dress with a white lace collar and a full skirt and she looks adorable. "You're always kissing Uncle Wade!" she accuses.

My cheeks go warm at being called out by a four year old.

"I really like Uncle Wade."

"I know," Autumn says in a voice that has clear *duh* undertones. "He likes you too. Maybe he likes you too much!"

With that declaration, she scampers off.

"You could never like me too much," I tell him, my gaze meeting his.

His eyes are serious though, making my smile fade. With gentle fingers he brushes the hair away from my forehead, making me tingle. "Maybe I don't just like you."

I part my lips, ready to say something funny in response but he beats me to the punch.

"Maybe I've fallen in love with you."

Oh. Oh my God. My heart starts racing and I swear my stomach feels like it just filled with about a million fluttering butterflies. "Maybe I've fallen in love with you too," I admit.

He smiles and it's the sweetest, most intimate smile I think I've ever seen on Wade's face. "Oh yeah? So we're in love now? Think the tabloids will buy it?"

I give him a little shove, then curl my fingers into the fabric of his sweater so I can tug him close. "Definitely," I murmur, just before I press my lips to his.

Bonus Scene!

Fable

"So."

I smile, barely able to contain my joy. "So."

It's way past midnight. We're in bed. The house is a semi disaster after the party, but I don't care. The children are finally asleep, but with our luck they'll wake us at six, eager to check under the tree to see what Santa Claus brought them.

Though I can't blame them for their excitement. I also can't wait to see their reactions to what Santa brought them. Growing up, Christmas had always been depressing for my family. Drew admitted his Christmases weren't that great either. So we go above and beyond to make our children's Christmas mornings extra special.

"I hear you have a surprise for me." Drew lifts a brow, his lips curled in the faintest smirk. "Spill woman."

I smile, thankful I kept my lamp on so I can see him. This

is my favorite time of day. When I can finally be alone with my husband, together in our giant bed. Sometimes we fall asleep fast. Sometimes we stay up and talk. Sometimes we have sex.

Okay, a lot of the time we have sex. I have to get as much naked Drew time as possible considering he's gone so much. The man is *busy*.

Though really, he's never too busy for me, or his children. He's a good man—a good husband. "What surprise are you talking about?" My innocent tone isn't working on Drew. He grabs hold of me and hauls me in close.

"The surprise you mentioned a few hours ago, when we snuck into the pantry and made out for ten minutes." Drew's lips brush against my forehead and I close my eyes, savoring our closeness, the busy-ness of today slowly catching up with me. I'm so tired.

But so incredibly happy.

"That was a pleasant Christmas Eve surprise," I tell him, because it so was. I'd been bustling around the kitchen, checking in on the caterer I hired when Drew magically appeared out of nowhere, snatched my hand and dragged me into the pantry.

Where he closed the door and proceeded to kiss me senseless. Surprisingly enough, no one had barged in and found us that entire time.

"I know. That was my plan." His hand runs up and down my back with just enough pressure to make me quietly moan. "Then you told me you had a surprise for me. That you'd tell me all about it later tonight."

Oh. That's right. I did say that. I was going to save it for Christmas day, but technically it already *is* Christmas day so I guess I should let him know.

"I went to the doctor a few days ago."

"Yeah? How did that visit go?" He can't always make my appointments and I know he hates that. But I understand. He's on the road a lot. I can't always expect him to be here. But when he is, he's fully present and with me and the kids as much as he possibly can be.

"Really good. I had an ultrasound," I say, my voice casual. "I know what sex the baby is."

He goes tense and he grabs hold of my arms, pulling away from me slightly so our gazes meet. "And you're only mentioning this to me now?"

"It was supposed to be a Christmas present." I pause. "That I was going to announce to the family when we're all sitting around the tree."

"You can go ahead and still do that," he tells me, his voice stern. "But don't you think I deserve to know what we're having before everyone else? I did have a part in this after all."

I burst out laughing. He's trying to sound mad, but he's teasing me. I can tell. "You played a part in this baby making thing? I had no idea."

"Right, right. I know I'm not around much, so you might forget who I am, but remember. I'm your husband." He pulls me into his arms once more, our gazes still locked. "I'm the one you make babies with. You're the mother of my children."

I know he's still playing around, but his words are making me emotional. Which is silly, I know it is, but I can't help it. The baby, the holiday season, being surrounded by family and friends, it's all messing with my fragile emotions and making me a wreck.

"So you don't want to wait to find out? I thought you might appreciate the anticipation."

"Give me a break." He's practically growling and I start to laugh, which is so much better than crying. "Boy or girl?"

"Guess."

Another growl. "You're torturing me."

"I know! It's so much fun." I run my hands all over his bare chest. He's hot, like a furnace, and he's wearing little clothing. This could get interesting real quick. "What do you want it to be?"

"I don't care as long as the baby is healthy and has your eyes." His expression is tender, a look he gives no one else but me. "Tell me, Fable. What are we having?"

Tears fill my eyes at his soft voice, the way he's looking at me, like I can do no wrong. "We're having another...girl."

He laughs and then he's kissing me, whispering against my lips. "I like girls. I like girls a lot. Autumn might be mad that she won't be the only princess, but she'll get over it."

"My macho quarterback doesn't want another boy so he can start forming his own personal football team?"

"You don't have to be a boy to join my football team," Drew says. "My girls are gonna be as tough as the boys, especially if they're like their mama."

I lightly smack his chest, but it's like smacking a brick wall. Pointless. He doesn't even flinch. He just smiles that dazzling Drew Callahan smile, though this one is more intimate. Just for me. Just for us. His blue eyes are warm, his big hands slowly stroking my skin. My heart flutters, my belly flutters, and I'm so incredibly thankful in this moment. That he can still make me feel this way.

But then worry comes in out of nowhere, swift and sure, and I look away from him, nibbling on my lower lip. "You're happy about this, right? About having another baby?"

His hands go still. "Fable. You can't be serious."

Nodding, I lift my gaze to his. "It's just so overwhelming sometimes—another baby. Now they'll out number us."

He chuckles. "Never thought of it that way before, but you're right. They might team up and take us down.

"You never know." I pull out of his arms and lie on my back, resting my hand on my still burgeoning belly. I get bigger faster with every child, I swear.

His hand joins mine on my stomach, sliding beneath the fabric of my thin T-shirt I wear to bed. "Another baby is a good thing." His voice is rich and deep, filled with emotion and when I glance up to find him watching me, my entire body starts to tremble.

"I think so too," I start to say but he cuts off the rest of my words with a kiss. It's slow and sweet, his tongue doing a thorough sweep of my mouth, his hands wandering all over my body. I give in to his touch, going willingly when he pulls me back into his embrace. I wind my arms around his neck, my hands going into his hair. The hold is familiar, we've done this a thousand times before, but it still feels so good, so incredibly right.

All these years later, marriage, kids, his successful career in the NFL, and these quiet, intimate moments with Drew never get old.

"You know, we haven't talked about how many children we want," he says long minutes later, after he's moved on to my neck. His voice is muffled against my skin, his words tickling me. "I guess we already know it's at least three."

Laughing, I tilt my head back, giving him better access. "Six?"

He lifts away from my neck to meet my gaze, a dumbfounded expression on his too handsome face. "Six?"

I nod. Don't say a word. I'm torturing him again. But that's okay. He can handle it.

"That's a lot." He hesitates. Swallows hard. "If you want six kids, I'll do my damnedest to give you six kids."

Ha. I'm sure he's referring to all the sex we'll need to have in order to knock me up three more times after this one. The perv.

Not that I'm protesting.

When it comes to Drew Callahan, I'll give him whatever he wants.

No questions asked.

Acknowledgements

I wrote this book for the readers who wanted Wade to have his own story. Remember Wade? Owen Maguire's best friend, the one character who has been mentioned in pretty much every single One Week Girlfriend book but didn't actually appear on the page until Four Years Later. I still get reader mail asking for his book.

So here it is.

I know his story isn't as angsty and heartbreaking as all the other books in the OWG series, but that's okay I think. Hopefully you think so too. In case you couldn't tell, I wrote this book for the Wade fans *and* for the Drew + Fable fans. Do you guys realize it's been four years since I released One Week Girlfriend? I remember how nervous I was to self publish that book. How fast I wrote it, how easy their story came to me, which doesn't always happen. How the book didn't sound like anything I'd ever written before so I decided to release it under another pen name (I'd been writing romance as Karen Erickson for years).

Monica Murphy kicked Karen's ass. One Week Girlfriend took off like a shot and changed my life—and my family's life too. Drew + Fable changed my career. I owe a lot to Drew + Fable. This means I also owe a lot to you, dear readers, for reading my books. So this one is for you.

I hope you enjoyed hanging out with Drew + Fable again. I didn't think they'd play such a central part in this book, but they almost took it over. My apologies. Though I don't think you'll complain too much.

A big, giant thank you to my assistant, Kati, my publicist Nina, my editor Mackenzie, my proofreader Dana, my formatter Emily and my cover designer Sarah. Thank you for helping me make this book the best it can be. Thank you to all the bloggers and reviewers for all your support over the years. Thank you to my family for being patient with me when I work too much.

And again, thank you to the readers. The last four years has been an exhilarating ride. Can't wait to see what's going to happen next.

I have a new series, and you can read the prequel (ONE NIGHT) for FREE at all retailers (include whatever retailer this book is formatted as) and on Wattpad <insert this link: https://www.wattpad.com/story/79420939-one-night>

There's a party over at Jordan Tuttle's house tonight and everyone is there. Including...

Olivia: Who's leaving for her dad's house in Oregon tomorrow. So she plans on having the time of her life tonight with her best friends.

Dustin: Who wishes Livvy could see just how much she means to him.

Emily: Who's trying her to best to get with someone. Anyone.

Cannon: Who has an encounter with Em he won't be able to forget.

Amanda: Who's finally ready to go all the way with her boyfriend.

Tuttle: Who discovers the girl he's always secretly liked just might like him back.

The first book, j u s t f r i e n d s, is available now!

It's the end of summer. Just before I start senior year with my two best friends in the whole world. Dustin and Emily are everything to me. We've been inseparable since middle school, and when we're together, nothing can go wrong.

But things aren't always what they seem. Em's turned into a drunken mess who parties too much. Dustin and I have hooked up a few times—and now he's ready to take our relationship to the next level. Yet I'm not sure I want things to change. I'm scared if I take it any further with Dustin, our friendship will be ruined forever. Then there's Ryan. The new guy. He's hot. He flirts way too much. And Em has totally set her sights on him.

So when my best friend betrays me in the worst possible way, guess who's there to help me pick up the pieces of my broken heart? Ryan. But he's so confusing. Annoying. Sweet. Sexy. I want to trust him, yet he makes it so hard. What I really want is for everything to go back to the way it was before.

Before I found out that best friends make the worst kind of enemies.

Read the first chapter for
just friends
on the next page!

chapter one

I miss you so much!
I miss you too.
I have a surprise for you.
What is it?
When you come home you'll find out.
But that's not until next week!
It's worth the wait. Trust me.
Does Dustin know the surprise?
Yes but he won't tell you.
How do you know?
Cuz he knows I'll kick his ass.

I stare at my phone screen, frustrated at my friend Emily's secrecy. She knows I hate surprises. I always have. Surprises usually bring bad news, at least for me.

Surprise! Pop quiz.

Surprise! You're failing Chemistry.

Surprise! He likes someone else.

Surprise! You're getting a baby brother.

Surprise! You're getting a baby sister.

Surprise! Your dad and I are getting a divorce.

Not necessarily in that order, but you get the gist.

Deciding to change tactics, I start texting Dustin.

What's up?

The usual. What's up wit u?

Bored. Lonely.

If you were here with me...

What?

I'd make sure you weren't bored.

Or lonely.

I smile, trying to fight the butterflies that flutter in my stomach when he talks like that. Dustin and I have been close since we were young. He's one of my best friends. I've told him everything. Confessed who I liked, who I'm mad at, how far I've gone with guys—which isn't very far—and he's admitted all his secrets too. He's the first person I got drunk with. The first person I got high with.

He's also the first boy I tongue-kissed. When we were thirteen and feeling like losers who'd never done anything, we at least had each other.

But it was forgotten. Kid stuff. Until last spring when we were at a party, got drunk together and started making out. Next thing I knew we were slipping our hands down each other's jeans, getting each other off. It happened again—and then again, right before I left for my dad's. I had to push him off of me before we took it too far.

I can still remember the pained expression on his face, and the memory of that night hurts my heart.

The memory also makes my heart flutter with excitement. Even though he's my best friend and I don't want to ruin our friendship, I can't help but wonder what would happen if we really were together. I trust Dustin. We're close without being in a relationship-close. I can also admit — only to myself — that Dustin is a good kisser. And he knows what to do with his fingers.

My cheeks are hot just remembering.

> **Where are you?**
> **In bed. Naked.**
> **Dustin...**
> **I know. Sorry.**

I chew on my lip, mad at myself for looking like a prude via text. The problem with messing around with your best friend who happens to be a boy is that they form certain expectations. We've crossed the line. In his eyes, there's no going back. He wants more. He wants it — me — all the time. I think I want that too, but I'm not sure.

> **What's Emily's surprise?**
> **I can't tell you.**
> **Why not?**
> **I was sworn to secrecy.**
> **Come on D.**

He doesn't answer and I don't push. But I'm frustrated. Being stuck at my dad's for the summer is the worst. Mom and Dad split when I was eleven and at first, being divided between two homes was awesome. I went to Dad's on the weekends and it was like one big party. We went out to eat, he bought me whatever I wanted, took me on trips. Summertime was even better. We'd go on vacations to the beach, or Disneyland, wherever I wanted to go. Birthdays I got twice as many gifts and the same with Christmas.

Mom's house, where I'm at most of the time, is the drag. Homework. Clean my room. Help out since she works and isn't always home to cook a decent meal. It's like a cycle set on repeat. *Do your homework, clean your room, do your laundry, help me, help me, help me.*

Dad's house was my escape. Until it wasn't.

He moved from California to Oregon for a new job and met and married Christine, who's much younger than my dad. Christine convinced him they should try for their own family. Now I have a little brother and sister named Dakota and Sierra—I know, I know, they sound like national parks— and trust me, they are a pain in my ass. Always getting into my stuff, always extra loud way too early in the morning.

No more epic summer vacations. I'm stuck in Oregon from mid-June to early August, where Dad works all day and Christine is at home, staring at me with obvious disappointment every time she spots me. So I hide away in my room, counting down the days until I can go back to Mom's.

At least at home, Mom doesn't really care what I do. As long as my room is clean, I help with chores, the homework is done and I come home by curfew, I can do pretty much whatever I want. She's rarely home anyway. Between her job as a nurse and her new boyfriend, she's busy. We talk on the phone once a week while I'm at Dad's and we occasionally text, but it's not the same.

I miss her when I'm not there and she drives me crazy when I'm home. But at least she's around more than Dad. He can't give me any time. He's too busy working or with Christine and his new kids, the better kids, the ones he wants to stick around for. Playing family man like it's some sort of show he's putting on for whoever's watching. I don't even know why I come here anymore, but Mom put a guilt trip on me, claiming this would be my last summer visiting Dad before I graduate high school.

She's right. So I'm suffering through one more summer before I can end this charade once and for all.

My phone buzzes and I grab it, reading the text from Dustin.

Check out E's IG.

I do as he says, scrolling through my feed. I've ignored Instagram pretty much the entire summer because looking at it makes me sad. Pics of my friends having fun back home while I'm stuck here with no social life? No thanks. I don't need to rub salt in the open wound.

But maybe Dustin's right and his request is a clue. Maybe Emily's account will show me the surprise.

I scroll and scroll, finally finding a photo of Emily with Dustin and another guy. A guy I don't recognize. Emily's standing in between them in a tiny lime green bikini, her skin red from the sun, chin-length dark brown hair tucked behind her ears and her lids lowered over her eyes at half mast, like she just took a hit or maybe she's drunk, the sloppy grin on her face confirming it. Probably both. She has a cup in her hand and the guy I don't know is looking at her like she's the best thing he's ever seen.

Huh. More like *he's* the best thing I've ever seen.

The caption below the photo says:

> *Summer daze make me feel good. #justfriends #friendzone #zoned #owned #relationship #lies #heartbreak #friends #bullshit*

I stare at the photo for a long time, then click on Emily's user name—crazysexycool4uuuu—so I can check out her other photos.

And there are a ton of them. The ones from late June show her in various swimsuits. Considering her parents are rich and she has her own credit card with a huge limit, she buys what she wants and damn the consequences. She looks good. Em's not curvy, but she's fit. In the eighth grade she played volleyball and softball. Gave that up once we got into high school because, and I quote, "I don't want anyone to think I'm some lezbo jock."

Politically correct and sensitive, that's my Em.

Early July photos show Em and her family visiting her grandparents, waving American flags and Em in a short video spelling her name out with a sparkler in her hand. Mid-July is Emily back at home, hanging with Dustin. Lots of photos of her and Dustin, always with their arms around each other, Dustin shirtless, Emily in a sexy bikini, their bodies pressed close.

Huh.

Frowning, I keep scrolling upward, since I went straight to June, wanting the surprise to ease up on me. Slow build, like the best kind of anticipation. But I'm starting to think there's no surprise at all. Unless she considers that guy in the photos the surprise.

Talk about lame.

Around July 19th is when I start to see the guy in her photos regularly. He's cute. Gorgeous really. Medium brown hair streaked with gold, sparkling light eyes — I can't tell if they're brown or green, or maybe they're hazel. Definitely not blue. Nice body, which I'm seeing a lot of since he appears shirtless in pretty much every photo. Most are taken by Em's pool and there are so many people there.

When did Em get so popular without me?

I close out Instagram and text Dustin.

> **Please don't tell me my surprise is the guy.**
> **More like he's E's surprise.**
> **What do you mean by that?**
> **They're hooking up. But he's a douche.**

I lean back against my pillows, stunned. I can hear my little brother and sister squealing downstairs. I hear a bird chirping just outside my window and the next-door neighbor is playing his radio outside as he gardens, some easy listening station that makes me want to stab pencils in my ears.

They're hooking up.

I'm a little…jealous? That guy is hot. And I'm also jealous over the photos with Em and Dustin. I miss them. I miss being a part of that friendship. The three of us against the world, it's always been like that. And it always hurts when one of us is missing.

Most of the time I'm the one missing.

You don't like him?

I sink my head farther into the pillows and close my eyes, waiting for Dustin's reply. Everything's changed this year. Last summer I was miserable and texting Em and Dustin every single day. And if we weren't texting we were calling each other, though that was rare. What we loved to do most was FaceTime each other and watch movies together. Simple stuff.

Innocent stuff.

Now I've seen Dustin's junk and he's seen my boobs and we've swapped spit. It's just all so…weird. Yet exciting. I sort of want to pursue more, but how do I tell him? How do we make this work without ruining everything? I don't want Em to feel left out either…

I hear my phone and I open my eyes, grabbing it.

He's okay. I guess Em needs the distraction.
What do you mean by that?

He doesn't reply for a while and I start to get nervous, nibbling on my thumbnail, feeling like an idiot for even asking.

I'll tell you when you come home. Hurry up. I miss you.

Aw. I miss him, too. A lot. We've known each other forever but grew extra close in fifth grade. I've been friends with Emily since middle school, when she first moved into the neighborhood. I love making friends with the new kids. It's like a hobby of mine, one that Dustin used to make fun of.

"You take in all the strays," he once teased me and I didn't protest because he was right.

Looks like Em took over my hobby this summer and made friends with the new boy.

My phone dings again and I look at the screen.

When are you coming home? Em wants to throw you a party.

I wrinkle my nose. I don't want a party.

> **Why? I don't need that sort of thing.**
> **That's her surprise. She's hanging with the popular crowd.**
> **Really?**
> **Yeah. They swim in her pool when her parents are at work.**

Huh. They're using her for her pool? That's lame. I'm surprised she'd let them. Most of the popular crowd at our high school can be rude. Snobbish. I'm on the yearbook staff so I have to deal with them a lot. Some are nice. I can't lump them all together as egotistical jerks, but a lot of them are. Em always agreed with me, saying she wanted real friends, not phony friends who only use each other.

Wonder when she changed?

more
than friends

is also available now!

He's not perfect, but he's all I want...

I'm your average girl at your average high school, trying to figure out my place in life. After catching my now ex-boyfriend messing around with my now ex-best friend, I've made some big changes. No more band, no more backstabbing friends and no more boring old life. Now I have new friends, a new job and new interests.

But there's a certain someone who's interested in me, and I don't get it. Jordan Tuttle could have anyone he wants. He's the most popular boy in school. Rich, gorgeous, smart and the star quarterback, he's perfect. Yet he acts like he wants no one else but...me. So despite my fears and doubt, I let him get close. Probably too close. I discover that he's not so perfect after all, but it doesn't matter. I'm falling for him, even though he runs so hot and cold. I know someday he's going to break my heart.

And I'm going to let him.

CPSIA information can be obtained
at www.ICGtesting.com
Printed in the USA
LVOW08s1509230117
521874LV00001B/271/P